PRAISE FOR SHION MIURA

PRAISE FOR *THE EASY LIFE IN KAMUSARI*

"Fans of all ages should enjoy the author's blend of the traditional and the contemporary . . . In a battle of Japanese settings, wondrous mountains win big over bustling cities."

—*Kirkus Reviews*

PRAISE FOR *THE GREAT PASSAGE*

Winner of an Earphones Award, Fiction

"Mastery of words may not result in masterly communication, and a great dictionary, like a love story, is 'the result of people puzzling over their choices'—a classic tension that has made *The Great Passage* a prizewinner in Japan, as well as both a successful feature film and an animated television series."

—*The New York Times*

"Swirling with witty enchantment, *The Great Passage* proves to be, well, utterly great. Readers should be advised to get ready to sigh with delighted satisfaction and awe-inspiring admiration."

—*Booklist* (starred review)

"*The Great Passage* has a philosophy of thoughtfulness and dedication to words that any reader will understand . . . Miura's prose—and Carpenter's translation—glide along, smooth and precise, with flashes of quiet poetry."

—*Metropolis*

"*The Great Passage* is interwoven with romantic love stories, but ultimately it is the passion of the characters, their friendship, and their devotion to their task that direct and complete the narrative and turn it from simply a good book to a great one."

—Talia Franks, Three Percent

KAMUSARI TALES TOLD AT NIGHT

ALSO BY SHION MIURA

Forest Series

The Easy Life in Kamusari

The Great Passage

KAMUSARI TALES TOLD AT NIGHT

BOOK 2 IN THE FOREST SERIES

SHION MIURA

TRANSLATED BY JULIET WINTERS CARPENTER

AMAZON **CROSSING**

Japanese names are written given name first.

Previously published as 神去なあなあ夜話 (*Kamusari Tales Told at Night*) by 徳間書店 / Tokuma Shoten in Japan in 2012 in care of Tuttle-Mori Agency, Inc., Tokyo. Translated from Japanese by Juliet Winters Carpenter. First published in English by Amazon Crossing in 2022.

Published by Amazon Crossing, Seattle

www.apub.com

Amazon, the Amazon logo, and Amazon Crossing are trademarks of Amazon.com, Inc., or its affiliates.

ISBN-13: 9781542039192 (hardcover)
ISBN-10: 1542039193 (hardcover)

ISBN-13: 9781542028882 (paperback)
ISBN-10: 1542028884 (paperback)

Cover design and illustration by Rex Bonomelli

Printed in the United States of America

First edition

KAMUSARI TALES TOLD AT NIGHT

1

THE FIRST NIGHT

THE ORIGIN OF KAMUSARI

Hey everybody! What's up? It's been a while—more than six months. Everybody doing okay? For all those who missed me so much you cried yourselves to sleep, you can dry those tears. I'm back!

I'm joking of course. *Everybody?* I'm sitting tapping this out on a computer that's not even connected to the internet. Yoki's place still has a black dial phone and that's it. For form's sake I'll go ahead and introduce myself. Pretending I'm writing for potential readers makes the sentences flow better.

My name is Yuki Hirano. I am the grandson of Lupin, the famous gentleman thief. No, that's not true. I just felt like writing it. My grandfathers were both salarymen, so no gentlemen thieves on either side. My old man works for a company in Yokohama. My mom's a homemaker.

The other day I turned twenty. Last spring, right after I graduated from high school, my life turned upside down. I left my folks' home in Yokohama (to be precise, I got thrown out), and I've been living here in Kamusari village ever since, deep in the mountains of midwestern Mie prefecture. If you want to know all about my upside-down life here, you'll have to read the other file in this computer, the one labeled "The Easy Life in Kamusari."

But you can't, because the computer is locked, and the password is secret. The contents of that file are so embarrassing, I don't want anybody eyeballing it. Especially Yoki. If he knew I was writing something, he'd laugh his head off: "Who do you think you are, Shakespeare?" That's why I sit at the computer in secret, at night.

What am I doing here in Kamusari, you ask? Forestry. I'm a woodsman. Every day I'm on a nearby mountain planting cedar or cypress saplings, cutting underbrush, pruning, or chopping timber and hauling it off. There's always lots to do.

For the first year I was a trainee, but this spring I became a full-time employee of Nakamura Lumber Co. Of course, I'm at the bottom of the pecking order.

Nakamura Lumber is run by Seiichi Nakamura, or "the master," as the villagers call him. Seiichi has good business sense, and he knows his stuff as a woodsman, too. Pretty impressive for someone still in his thirties. His family has owned mountains around Kamusari going back generations. After the industry began to decline, they sold some of them, but even so he owns enough to fill Tokyo Dome 256 times over. In the old days, the scale of their holdings was so vast, you could go from Mie all the way to Osaka and never leave Nakamura land.

We work in teams. Seiichi is my team leader, and we mostly tend the forests on his land. The other teams in Nakamura Lumber work with the Forestry Union or hire themselves out to people who are too old to work their own land.

Now I'll introduce the members of the Nakamura team. I've already told you about our leader, Seiichi. There's also his childhood friend Yoki Iida, a big, brawny guy in his early thirties with short hair he dyes yellow. Yoki's always bragging about what a genius he is at forestry, and as much as I hate to admit it, he's right. Using just an ax, he can fell a tree with pinpoint control. His personality is another story. He's uninhibited, you could say. Reckless. Goes strictly by instinct.

Then there's Iwao Tanabe, who's in his fifties, and Saburo Koyama, who's in his late seventies and still going strong. Everybody calls him Old Man Saburo. Iwao has the glorious distinction (?) of having been spirited away by the god of Mt. Kamusari when he was a little kid. He's really knowledgeable about every aspect of forestry, and he patiently explains things to me. Old Man Saburo knows everything there is to know about mountains and forests. Also, he's got an amazing ability to smell trouble. If Old Man Saburo says, "Maybe we'd better be headin' back," then no matter how blue the sky looks, we clear out. And nine times out of ten, by the time we get back to the village, there'll be a thunderstorm. It's not safe to be on a mountain during a thunderstorm because of the risk of lightning. Even Wild Man Yoki listens to Old Man Saburo.

So everybody on the Nakamura team is an expert woodsman. Everybody but me. Still, I'm gradually getting used to the work. At first, walking up a slope or cutting underbrush, I could hardly stand up straight, and I had a hard time climbing trees to cut off branches, too. Sometimes when I used my chain saw to fell a cedar, I'd get the blade wedged in the trunk at a funny angle and no matter what I did, it wouldn't come out. Compared to those days, I'm a regular *tengu* now. Well, not an actual tengu, one of those half man, half bird spirits of the mountain in folklore. But I can move around gracefully on the slopes, shimmy up and down trees, cut underbrush, prune, and pretty much handle what comes my way. Felling trees is the one thing I still have to work on. Yoki teases me: "Tell me when you're about to cut down a tree and I'll get out of the way, like a mile away."

Iwao cautions me nearly every day: "When you start feeling like you've got the hang of things, that's when you're most in danger. Don't let yourself get complacent." I know he's right. The work is hard; nobody could master it in just a year or two. I learn something new every day, and since we work close to danger, I always have to think about what I'm doing. Sometimes I feel both physically and mentally on the verge of collapse. And yet it's fun.

When we're on the mountain, birdsong echoes through the trees. Bushes sway, and I can sense animals watching us. Every step on the forest floor's soft soil releases a moist, sweet smell. During a break, when I wash my face in the stream, the water is cold and so pure it feels like it'll soak right into my skin. The breeze is clear and smooth, not a grain of dust in it. (Except for pollen season.)

There's nothing in Kamusari. No place to hang out, no convenience store, no clothing store, no restaurant. Nothing but mountains on every side, layer on layer, covered in green. But the experiences I've had here are unlike any I could have had in Yokohama. Village life was hard on me at first, but before I knew it, forestry had a hold on me.

I live at Yoki's house. When I was promoted to full time, I thought about renting a place of my own. The village population is declining, so there are plenty of old houses standing empty. But then I'd have to buy furniture and wheels, which I can't afford yet, so I decided to go on taking advantage of Yoki's hospitality. Besides, I want to observe him and learn all I can, steal from him to improve my skills. He's really particular about keeping his tools in shape, for one thing, and really good at it. Which is funny because he's hopeless at everything else around the house. Can't sew on a button for the life of him, and about all he can make in the kitchen is miso soup.

Yoki lives with his Granny Shige and Miho, his wife. His parents died young. Their photos and mortuary tablets are displayed on the family Buddhist altar. They look to be in their forties, and they're smiling. Quiet, decent people, as far as I can tell. How they managed to give birth to a wild creature like Yoki, I'll never know. The altar always has offerings of rice, water, flowers, and incense, but Yoki has never said anything to me about his folks.

Granny Shige is very old and can't walk much. She mostly sits in the family room looking like a wrinkled bean-jam bun, but she has unerring judgment based on her lifetime of experience. The villagers all look up to her. If she has to, she'll move like lightning and give Yoki a good hard smack on the forehead to punish him for something he's done. "Feels like my forehead's giving off smoke," he told me. Yoki generally behaves himself around Granny Shige.

Yoki and Miho have been married for years, but they're still in love. She's so smitten, sometimes she gets crazy jealous. Once, after Yoki spent some time at a hostess bar in Nabari, she got so mad she went home to her parents. Of course, they live less than a five-minute walk away, just beyond the bridge, in the back of the only store in Kamusari district: a little earthen-floor place with assorted necessities.

There's one other important member of the family I forgot to mention, and that's Noko. He's a shaggy white dog, as smart as can be and Yoki's faithful buddy. He goes along with us to the mountains. Also, Granny Shige has two goldfish. Normally they swim around peacefully together in their glass bowl, but when she sprinkles food on the water, they lunge at it like piranhas.

Every morning, I go to the mountains in Yoki's pickup truck. Noko rides along in the flatbed. Lunch is *onigiri* that Miho makes, one for each of us. There's nothing else, but her onigiri are huge, three cups of rice each, and stuffed with goodies: croquettes, even, as well as pickled radish and pickled plum. When Yoki is fooling around with other women, the contents dwindle one by one until we're left with a big ball of rice flavored only with salt. In the end, she won't make even that. So I keep an eagle eye on Yoki, and every day I pray to the gods of Kamusari to keep that marriage happy.

Now I've finally come to my main topic. Tonight I want to write about the gods of Kamusari. When I was a trainee, I wrote about what I saw and heard on the mountains and what was going on in the village. There's a reason why I decided to start writing again after letting it slide for months. I heard an interesting story, and that gave me an idea. Why not record village legends, stories about the villagers, and other items I come across? Pretty cool idea, I think. It shows I've gotten more used to the work and to village life. I can relax a bit.

The other day, we went to work as usual and came back earlier than planned. "Those are thunderclouds," Old Man Saburo said, and sure enough, just as we got down off the mountain, a storm hit. The rain was coming down so hard that even with the windshield wipers going full force, we could hardly make out anything in front of us. The thunder was fierce. I was sitting in the passenger seat, holding poor Noko on my lap. A cataract poured down the windshield, and as the wipers cleared it away, I caught a glimpse of a bolt of lightning connecting the top of West Mountain to the sky. Almost simultaneously, there was a gigantic clap of thunder. Noko panicked and clawed his way up from my lap to my chest and even my face. Those claws of his are sharp.

Yoki knows the mountain roads backward and forward, and he's an ace driver (he's good at anything that requires sharp reflexes), so we made it home in one piece. Iwao's pickup almost skidded into the river. But the villagers are philosophical about such things. Nobody showed any alarm when Iwao said afterward, "My rear wheels spun. Had a close call." They just smiled and said, *"Naa-naa."* Somebody drawled, "Bound to happen in a torrent like that."

Naa-naa is a common expression in Kamusari village. It's used in various ways to mean "Let's take our time," "Relax, calm down," or even "Nice day today, isn't it?" In this case, while conveying the nuance of "Gee, that's tough," it meant, "In the end nothing happened, so let it go." Kamusari dialect has its own flavor. I still haven't mastered it, so you'll have to kind of use your imagination as you go along.

Anyway, we made it safely home. Yoki and I took turns soaking in the old-fashioned iron tub—the kind named *goemon*, after a notorious thief who was executed by being boiled alive—and by the time I put some disinfectant on my nose where Noko had scratched it, the rain had stopped. In late September, the weather is really unpredictable. It's as if summer and winter are competing in the sumo ring of fall, battling to see which is stronger. Storms are pretty frequent.

Yoki and I sat talking in the family room. "I wonder if West Mountain's all right," I said. "I thought I saw smoke coming from a tree hit by lightning."

"Nothin' to worry about," Yoki said. "The trees are wet with rain, so lightning couldn't start a forest fire."

Miho made a pot of tea, and Granny Shige sliced some red bean jelly from the cabinet. The four of us sat on tatami around the low, round table, sipping tea and eating jelly. Noko lay sprawled on the earthen floor in the entryway, wagging his tail weakly. The thunderstorm must have really freaked him out, because he wouldn't go to his doghouse in the yard.

Drops of water plopped quietly from tree branches into puddles on the ground. Birds cried noisily, seeking a place to roost for the night. The breeze felt chilly and moist. I got up to shut the sliding glass door and went out onto the veranda. Gray clouds were scudding east.

Just then, Santa came into the yard, wearing yellow boots. "Hey, Santa, what's up?" I said. Santa is Seiichi's little boy. Just started first grade this spring. (His name means "mountain man" and has nothing to do with Christmas, just so you know.)

The village is divided into three districts: Shimo, Naka, and the one where we live, Kamusari. Santa is the only school-age kid in our district, so he goes to Kamusari Elementary in Naka district. Even though it's in the same village, it's a forty-minute walk on a steep road. That's too much for a first grader, so Santa takes the bus. There's a community bus that serves the village, morning and evening, mainly so old folks can get to town. Every morning on the bus, the elderly passengers fuss over him. "They give me tons of candy and crackers!" he once told me, beaming.

First grade lets out early, long before the evening bus, so Santa hoofs it home, going with his friends partway. Sometimes when the weather's bad, his mother, Risa, drives down to pick him up. So yeah, mountain life has its inconveniences. But to Santa this is all completely normal. Doesn't bother him one bit. He seems to like going to school.

Anyway, Santa came into the yard, and when he saw me standing on the veranda his face lit up.

"You're home early 'cause of the rain, right, Yu-chan?" he said. "I thought you would be. Now that school's started, I'm pretty busy and I don't get to see you much, so I thought I'd come over and say hi."

Cheeky little bugger. But Santa looks up to me. Like he said, we hadn't spent much time together lately, and I guess he missed me. I have to say I was pretty glad to see him, too.

"Sure. C'mon in."

Santa went in through the front door, patted Noko, and called out politely, "Hello, it's me, Santa," before stepping up into the family room. Miho poured him a cup of tea, and Granny Shige cut him a nice big slice of bean jelly.

"Hey there, Santa." Yoki, who'd been lying down with his head on a wicker wastebasket for a pillow, sat up. "You here alone? Where's your daddy?"

"He turned in early. He said to tell you he's gonna check out West Mountain tomorrow."

"Got it. Here you go, sit yourself down." Yoki handed over the cushion he had been sitting on, and Santa plopped down on it, right between Yoki and me. He said a proper thank-you before starting on the bean jelly. Nothing wrong with his manners.

"Did you get caught in the rain, Santa?" asked Miho.

"Nope. I made it home just in time."

"You lucked out," said Yoki. "That's 'cause you're a good boy. The river might flood, so don't go near it tonight or tomorrow, okay?"

Santa nodded.

Granny Shige had been sitting quietly, working her mouth, but all of a sudden, she spoke up: "Once upon a time, all Kamusari lay under water."

"Are you all right, Granny Shige?" I asked, half-afraid she was picking up signals from the world beyond.

"Right as rain. I'm about to tell the legend of Kamusari."

"Oh, okay. By all means, please do."

Why she suddenly took it into her head to tell the old tale, I have no idea, but I turned to face her expectantly. Everybody else was sitting up straight, too, and all eyes were glued on her, even though everybody but me must have heard the story more times than they could count. There isn't a lot of entertainment in Kamusari village, so I guess Granny Shige telling an old tale is a pretty big deal.

Long ago, back before the name Kamusari existed, there used to be a great big lake here. Mt. Kamusari was half underwater. Gods lived on the mountains, and in the lake, too, of course. People—our ancestors—lived in little huts on the mountainside, scraping out a living as best they could by gathering nuts, hunting wild boar, and making charcoal.

When a wind swept down from the mountain, the surface of the lake would shimmer and ripple. When people saw the ripples shining like fish scales, they whispered to each other that the god of the lake was tickling the wind. The god of the lake was a big white snake.

One year, it was cold all summer, and in the fall, the nuts stayed small and never did turn brown. People and birds and animals all wasted away, and over the winter many of them died. When spring came, the people who had managed to survive made an appeal to the god of the lake.

"Snake god," they said, "at this rate we'll all starve and disappear. Please make the lake go away. Then there will be level land that we can use to grow rice and vegetables, so we can lay in stores for ourselves for the winter. Naturally, we'd offer some to you, too."

The snake god heard this, coiled at the bottom of the lake, and he was troubled. Getting rid of the lake would mean giving up his home. He stuck his head out of the water and looked at the people gathered on the shore, their palms pressed together in supplication.

Standing among them was a beautiful girl, the only daughter of the village head—but this was before there was a village, so let's call him the tribal chieftain. The girl's hair was jet black, her skin was snow white, and her lips were red as red could be. She was prettier than any camellia on the mountain, more bursting with life than any fish in the lake, young and lovely.

One look and the snake god lost his heart to her. So he said, "I'll grant your request. In exchange, I want the chieftain's daughter for my bride."

Nobody was more surprised than the girl and her parents. God or no god, who would want to be the wife of a snake? The parents would have turned the offer down cold, but the girl had a tender heart. She couldn't ignore other people's suffering.

"Very well," she said. "If you make the lake go away, I will be your wife."

That night, a loud rumbling came from the lake. The people sleeping in their little huts leaped up, but it was pitch-dark, and they couldn't see a thing. They waited restlessly for dawn. When they looked out in the light of morning, they were amazed.

The lake was gone. In its place was a clear river surrounded by rich, flat earth. The people came down from the mountain and settled where the lake used to be. The place still had no name, but that became our village of Kamusari, and the river that the snake god made was our Kamusari River.

"What happened to the snake god after that?" asked Santa. This didn't seem to be the first time he was hearing the story, but his eyes were bright with interest.

"That's the heart of the story," Granny Shige said solemnly. "Just listen."

When the lake disappeared, so did the snake god. The first year, the villagers offered him some of the rice and vegetables they harvested, but by and by they forgot there'd ever been a lake, let alone a snake god. Their lives were easier than before, and they forgot all about their promise.

But one person didn't forget—the daughter of the tribal chieftain. Every day, she thanked the snake god and worried about his safety. Her parents brought her one marriage proposal after another, but she turned them all down and waited to be married to the snake god.

One night, a young fellow came in secret to see her. His name was Nagahiko, and oh, he was a fine figure of a man. "I've always loved you," he said, and pressed his case hard. She soon gave in to him, and, without telling her parents, she and Nagahiko became as husband and wife.

"That's good," said Santa. "Nagahiko was really the snake god, right?"

I'd been suspecting the same thing, but jeez, Santa, I thought, *wait for it; don't give away the ending!* I glared at him, but my disapproval didn't seem to register.

"Was he handsome?" he asked Granny Shige.

"He was a god, wasn't he? Of course he was handsome."

"Like Daddy?"

"I suppose he was as good-looking as Seiichi. One thing's for sure: he didn't look like a hoodlum like Yoki here."

"Hey!" said Yoki. "Seiichi and I are different types, but I'm good-looking, too." He ran a hand through his bright yellow hair,

11

sulking, as Miho looked on in amusement. Paying him no mind, Granny Shige went on with her story.

Nagahiko came to see the girl every night but always slipped away before dawn. The girl started to worry, because by then she was deeply in love. She started to think Nagahiko might be seeing another woman in the daytime, and that made her jealous.

I interrupted. "Should you be telling a story like this in front of Santa?" I sneaked a peek at Miho, who raised jealousy to a fine art.

Miho leaned across the table and scolded me: "Be quiet, the best part's coming!"

Whether Santa understood or not, he was smiling. I gave up and said no more. My legs had started to go to sleep under me, so I changed my position and sat cross-legged, ready for the rest of the story.

The girl confessed to her parents that a young man was coming to see her every night. Astonished at this news, her parents gave her a ball of hemp thread. "Tie one end to the hem of his kimono," they said, "and in the morning, follow it and see where it leads. That way, you can find out where he lives."

And she did. The man tore himself away from her and left before morning, never knowing she'd attached a thread to the hem of his kimono. As the thread spooled out, the ball got smaller and smaller in her hand. She ran and got another ball of thread, but pretty soon that one was used up, too. In all, it took seven balls before the thread stopped unwinding.

When morning light shone on the village, the girl and her parents set off down the road, following the thread across the bridge, along the river, and up into the mountain. It was the highest of all the mountains around the village, the one where a god named Oyamazumi was said to live. The mountain was sacred, so people hardly ever set foot there.

"It was Mt. Kamusari!" cried Santa in glee. "What happened then? Was Nagahiko on Mt. Kamusari?"

"Now, don't rush me." Granny Shige drank some tea. "Yes, Nagahiko was on Mt. Kamusari. With his lake gone, he'd moved in with Oyamazumi. He was lying fast asleep, in the form of a white snake."

The snake god soon realized humans were nearby and looked up. There in front of him were the girl he loved and her parents, all of them round-eyed in amazement. He said to her with resignation, "You found me out. I loved you so much I took on lowly human form to be with you at night, but now that you've seen my true form, we can't be together anymore. You wouldn't want a snake for a husband. It grieves me to say so, but this is goodbye."

Trembling, the girl slowly approached him and flung her arms around his neck. "No!" she cried. "I love you, too. I don't want us to part. Besides, with your lake gone, what will you do? Marry me, the way you promised, and come live with me in the village. Together we can till the field and gather nuts and be happy. All right?"

The snake god nodded. They hugged each other—he coiled himself right around her—and sobbed for joy. The snake god was overjoyed because the girl still loved him even after seeing him in his true form, and the girl was overjoyed because the snake god still wanted her even at the sacrifice of his old home.

And so they lived together in the village as man and wife—or beast and wife, or god and wife. And they were happy ever after.

"Good." Santa sounded satisfied.

I could hardly keep from laughing. To hear Granny Shige tell it, that snake god spoke perfect Kamusari dialect. Funny way for a god to talk, if you ask me.

It was already dark outside. A voice sounded at the front door.

"May I come in?" The door opened, and in stepped Risa. "Sorry if Santa's being a bother."

"Mommy!" Santa flew down into the entryway. Noko wagged his tail.

Miho followed Santa and went on into the kitchen to start supper. "Santa," she said, "will you stay and eat with us?"

"Not today. I'll go home. Granny Shige, thanks for the story. Yu-chan, wanna go fishing in the river sometime?"

"You bet. But let's wait till the water level goes down."

"Okay."

Santa went home with Risa, who'd brought over a Tupperware container filled with piping hot, simmered sweet potatoes and deep-fried tofu. Yoki and I helped ourselves while we drank sake. He drank his in a glass tumbler, but I poured mine into a little sake cup and sipped it. I'm still not that used to drinking alcohol.

Noko must have cheered up, because he was asking to be let outside. I took him out, filled his dish with dog food, and gave him some water. The rain clouds were gone, and the sky twinkled with stars. It was too dark to make out the outline of Mt. Kamusari, home of the god Oyamazumi.

The smell of wet leaves. Rustle of dark mountain forests in the wind. Sharp, clean air filled with insect cries, some like wind chimes, others like the grinding of a pestle. As I stood there in the night, the legend that this was once the bottom of a huge lake began to seem real. It felt entirely possible that somewhere on Mt. Kamusari was a giant white snake, zigzagging across the mountainside, its body twisting like lightning.

When I went back inside, supper was ready. Besides the usual hot white rice and homemade turnip pickles, there was miso soup with tofu and scallions, boiled spinach, and grilled horse mackerel.

With Santa gone, the house was awfully quiet. The only sound was the ticking of the wall clock.

"I liked that story you told, Granny Shige," I said. "Marrying a snake is kinda weird, though."

"Happened all the time, long ago." She was unfazed. "That story was handed down in Seiichi's family."

Yoki laughed. "Then he's descended from the snake god."

What if Seiichi changed shape in the early morning as he slept? Picturing Santa lying asleep between Risa and a big white snake, I laughed, too.

I asked Miho for more rice, and then said, "One thing has always bothered me. Kamusari means 'god departed.' How did the village ever get a name like that? Isn't it unlucky?"

"You'll understand when you hear the rest of the story," Miho said, passing me back my bowl piled high with rice. "Granny Shige, why not tell him?"

"All right." Granny Shige has no teeth, so she was chewing a turnip pickle with her gums. She's got really strong gums. "This part is for adult ears only, but Yuki's all grown up now, so I can tell him." And so she finished the story.

The girl and Nagahiko built a little house and tilled a little field, and they were happy. They shared a futon every night, and fourteen children were born to them. Seven were born in the form of a little white snake, and in time they all left the village to become protective gods of ponds and marshes all around.

The other seven were born in human form, and they worked hard and were a blessing to their parents. When the girls grew up, they married happily into farming families in neighboring villages or across the mountain. The boys all took wives, and their families grew and prospered.

The girl—I'll go on calling her that, though of course she was no girl anymore, but a mother many times over—she and Nagahiko were as much in love as ever. Until he met her, he'd never known a woman's flesh. Only after meeting the girl did he know the warmth of skin on skin. In short, Nagahiko was addicted to lovemaking.

He had taken human form in order to live with the girl in the village, but when he was in her arms, he sometimes felt like he'd gone back to being a snake. He'd look down at himself in surprise, but no, he wasn't a snake. Well, all but one part of him, that is. When that snakelike part of him burrowed inside the girl, Nagahiko was reminded of the lake where he used to live. His beautiful clear lake, so quiet, so warm, so safe.

Time went by, and the girl got old. But Nagahiko was no different from the first time he appeared before her. Gods never age and never die, so he didn't know what was happening. The girl was sick at heart, knowing she had to die and leave him and that he wouldn't understand, being a stranger to death. With his old lake gone, the only place in the world where he truly belonged was at her side. Now she had to go away and leave him to fend for himself among the villagers.

From her deathbed, she said in tears, "I've loved you with all my heart, but now it's time for me to go. Even if I'm not here, I want you to keep on living in this village in peace and good health."

"Where are you going?" Nagahiko said in surprise, taking her wrinkled hand in his. "I'll go with you."

"You can't come. You're a god, and I'm a human. For a while we were able to share a life here in the village, but now we must go our separate ways."

Those were her last words. Her eyes closed, and no matter how the snake god called to her, she said no more. Still he wouldn't give up. For seven days and seven nights he sat right beside her. Her flesh grew cold and hard, and by and by it gave off the stench of decay. Only then did he realize that never again would she open her eyes, or talk, or smile.

The snake god changed back into the form of a great snake and swallowed the girl's body whole. He did it to stay close to her—but her body was only flesh. Her spirit had flown away.

The villagers froze with fear to see a great white snake come crawling out of the house. The snake didn't give them a glance. He slid into the river and swam upstream, toward the highest mountain. He crawled around the mountain, crying out and weeping. He thrashed so wildly that all the trees on the mountain shook, and some of them toppled over.

Oyamazumi didn't know what to do. "What makes you so sad, Nagahiko?" he asked. "Tell me."

"My wife went away, and I miss her terribly." The snake god had cried so many tears that he was drained. His scales were parched.

"Oh, is that the trouble? Then the answer is simple," said Oyamazumi. "Go find yourself a new wife."

The snake god decided to follow this advice. He wriggled down the mountain, swam downstream in the river, and went back to the village, where once again he took the form of Nagahiko, the handsome young man.

A girl in the village fell in love with him at first sight. She invited him to her house, and they made love. Just like the girl who'd been his wife, this girl, too, had a clear lake inside her, where the snakelike part of him just fit.

But the snake god knew right away that something wasn't right. This girl's lake was clear, but not quiet and warm and safe. He couldn't understand it. Confused and disappointed, he turned himself back into a snake. The girl screamed and ran away.

After that Nagahiko made love to other girls, but the result was always the same. The lake never made him feel quiet and warm and safe, and the girl always screamed and ran away.

Pleasures of the flesh lost their appeal for him. Then he understood: the girl he married had said she loved him with all her heart, and he'd loved her with all his heart, too. That must be what human lovemaking was *all about. If you didn't truly love the other person, you couldn't enjoy true pleasure with them.*

The snake god went back up to the highest mountain and said to Oyamazumi, "I've been around here a long time, seeing how humans live. I even took a human wife and lived with her in the village. Now the village is full of my children and grandchildren."

"That's very good." Oyamazumi nodded. "And did you find yourself a new wife?"

"No. My wife's gone. Other girls are made the same way she was, but they're not her. I think I grew a heart. My wife helped my heart to grow, and without her, no matter who I make love to, it's not the same."

"That's a shame."

"Marrying a human brings sorrow. I'm lonely and miserable in the village."

"What are you going to do?"

"I thought I'd go someplace where there are no humans around. It's been so long, I can hardly remember, but weren't we born somewhere else?"

"We were indeed. Somewhere far away, I have a feeling, beyond the sky."

"I'm going to find my way back there and rest my bones, remembering my marriage. But I have a favor to ask of you, Oyamazumi-san."

"What's that?"

"I want you to keep watch over the village and the villagers. My descendants are there, for one thing, but the others are good people, too. Help them live in peace, will you?"

"How can I say no to you, my old friend? I'll watch over them all right. Leave it to me. Go on your way and don't worry about a thing."

"Thanks. That means a lot to me. Then I'll be off. Goodbye."

"Take care."

Leaving the future of the village in Oyamazumi's hands, the snake god took off from the top of the mountain, heading for his old home beyond the sky.

And ever since, that mountain has been called Mt. Kamusari, the river has been called the Kamusari River, and the village where we live has been called Kamusari village. Oyamazumi protects us, just as he promised the snake god he would. He'll keep on doing it, too, but only if we believe in him. Now that's all there is, there isn't any more!

"However many times I hear it, that story always gets to me. It's heart-breaking." Miho squirmed.

I cocked my head, considering. "What happened to the girls the snake god dumped?"

"Oh, after bedding a god they'd have been the toast of the town." Yoki grinned. "They had distinction. You can bet they all married village boys."

"I wonder." The snake god's behavior bothered me. Plus he went and swallowed his wife's dead body. *Eww.*

"Yoki, you don't get it!" Miho flared up. "What matters in the story is that two people can't truly enjoy pleasure together unless they're in love!"

"That's the point of the story?"

"Yes! Right, Granny Shige?"

"Yep. It's ages now since I had pleasure with my husband, but what we had was fine, all right." She looked blissful, remembering bygone days, or nights.

Sheesh. What's with these oversexed people?

"For a young guy, Yuki, you seem kind of take-it-or-leave-it," said Yoki disapprovingly. "At this rate, you'll never get it on with Nao."

Come on. What a thing to say!

Nao is the girl I'm wild about. She's Risa's little sister, and she teaches at Kamusari Elementary. Unfortunately, she's got a big crush on Seiichi and has no eyes for me. I've been doing my best, inviting her out on my days off, but I haven't made much progress.

19

But that's okay. I mean, it's not like I've never had a girlfriend before. With Nao, I plan to take it slow, get to know her gradually.

Nao is different from any other girl I've ever known. How, exactly, I couldn't tell you, but she is. When she smiles at me, it's as if my soul is floating over a mountain in spring. When she gets mad, she's as pretty as a mountain wrapped in fall colors, and when she comes out with a strong opinion, she has the charm of a snowcapped mountain in winter. Charming yet unapproachable—she's like a winter mountain that way, too.

And when I encounter her tenderness, it's as if the cool breeze from a mountain in summer is caressing my cheek. I close my eyes and want to fill my lungs with that transitory breeze, make it mine.

I'm kind of a poet, hey? Love has made poetry spring again in my heart. When I was in high school, I secretly wrote a *Book of My Poems*. Don't tell.

Yoki, Miho, and Granny Shige are all asleep. I spent the last three nights writing in the six-mat room they gave me. Gosh, I wrote a lot. Tomorrow morning I've got work, so I'd better get to bed.

This chapter is all about how Kamusari village came to be. What do you think? Who'd have imagined that in ancient times the village was entirely underwater? Come to think of it, with mountains all around, this would be the perfect place for a dam. But no—if there were a dam here, there'd be nowhere to live.

As for the part about Seiichi being descended from the snake god, or the snake god having a passionate marriage and then wandering about in search of physical pleasure, I don't know what to say. But it's a legend pulsing with life, fit for a village of people who take life easily, unfazed by whatever comes their way.

There's one other thing that leaves me at a loss for words, and that's Yoki and Miho. The night Granny Shige told the legend of the snake god, I could hear them making passionate love in their room. I wish to heck they'd cut it out. Paper doors are all that separates their room from mine! Meanwhile, Granny Shige was sleeping like a log—a log that snores. Only she could have slept through the racket they were making.

I tiptoed out and went to the bathroom. Then, instead of going back to bed, I went out and sat on the veranda. Noko heard me and left his doghouse to join me. I patted his neck and looked up at the sky. It wasn't cold enough to see my breath, but the air was chilly and clear. A staggering number of stars was overhead, blazing away as usual. From off in the distance came the rustle of trees on the mountains.

What's Nao doing now? I wondered. Maybe she had finished preparing tomorrow's lessons and gone to bed. Or could she be watching TV as a distraction? There are only a handful of channels to choose from. I felt like calling her, but cell phones here work only high in the mountains. Hard to believe, huh?

With no phone, I can't text her or send an email. Using the house landline in the middle of the night doesn't seem like a good idea, either. So on nights when I just want to hear her voice, all I can do is think about her. Send her my love, with all my might. Wouldn't want to give her nightmares, though, so mentally I shout *I love you!* for about ten seconds and then stop.

Sitting alone on the veranda, I wondered if the snake god made it safely beyond the sky. Was he still "resting his bones" and clinging to memories of his dead wife? Gods might not have a sense of time, but it must have been lonesome for him with only memories for comfort. Still, I felt sure he had no regrets—wasn't a bit sorry he took a human wife and, in Granny Shige's phrase, "enjoyed true pleasure" with her. I bet he was glad he had encountered humans and lived happily amid our mortality for a time.

Yoki slid open the floor-length window to his room. "We're through," he said, like it was a big deal. "Sorry to keep you up."

"Miho's asleep?"

"Yeah." He smiled smugly.

Stop looking like the cat who ate the canary. I want to hurry and rent a house where I can live by myself. Of course, if I could live there with Nao, so much the better.

I pretended to give Yoki a swift kick and went back inside.

Man, I really have to get to bed. I'll stop here for tonight. If something else comes up I want to write about, I'll be back. We're heading into winter, and when it snows, there won't be as much to do. I'll be able to come around often, so don't cry, baby.

Who am I kidding? Nobody's reading this.

Till next time!

2

THE SECOND NIGHT

LOVE IN KAMUSARI VILLAGE

It's October now, and winter will soon be setting in. Everybody feeling good? (That last line to be read in the boisterous style of pro-wrestler-turned-lawmaker Antonio Inoki.)

Tonight I have good news and bad news. Which do you want to hear first?

Doesn't that question kind of rub you the wrong way? Like this Q and A at a group blind date:

"How old are you?"

"How old do you think I am?"

In the first place, don't ask such a dumb question. In the second place, don't be coy about a dumb question.

Since I'm in love with Nao, I might be especially sensitive about that particular Q and A. She's five or six years older than me, and she definitely makes more money than I do. So sometimes I feel at a distinct disadvantage. But here in Kamusari, a group blind date seems like something from another planet. Nao and I are the only young singles in the whole village. A group blind date is out of the question. She and I would be the only participants. Period. Wouldn't work.

Come to think of it, the last time I went on a group blind date was the winter of my senior year in high school. That means it's going on two years since I've made out with a girl. It's tough. Sometimes I feel like I might explode down there. Not that writing about it here helps any.

Enough about group blind dates. It's a custom from an alien planet anyway. So without any coy "How old do you think I am?"–style playing around, I'll get on with my story. I'll write about what I want, at the pace I want. Because this is no group blind date. I'm sitting all alone at the computer, typing. The emptiness of it wrenches my heart . . .

I'll pull myself together and start with the good news. I, Yuki Hirano, twenty years old, just got my driver's license! Yay! (Applause.) I still can't drive a forklift or pilot a ship. It's for ordinary passenger cars. But now I can go wherever I want. I can even invite Nao out for a drive. Though since I haven't got a car, I'd have to borrow Yoki's pickup.

"Sorry to keep you waiting, Nao. Also, sorry, these are Yoki's wheels, but anyway, hop on in."

How would that be, I wonder? What would she think of someone who showed up for a date in someone else's vehicle—a pickup truck, no less? I'm pretty sure she doesn't care about stuff like that, but I do. It's petty, I know, but I can't help thinking that Nao couldn't be very impressed by someone who's younger than her, doesn't make as much money, and doesn't even own a car, which is a necessity here.

I'm a small person who sits around brooding about things like this. Although I decided . . . well, I'll tell the whole story and lead up to my decision naturally. My name means "courage," so I'll live up to my name, show some courage, and ask her boldly!

Where was I? Ah, yes. Nao told me I'm "small." It was a shock. Not that I showed her my manhood, mind you. I think I'm normal-sized there. But maybe the fact that my mind immediately veers in that

24

direction just shows how small I really am. Gah. What am I supposed to do?

Time for the bad news, everybody. You may have guessed it already, but the truth is, Nao and I had a fight. Let me explain.

I couldn't wait to see her, so I walked. It takes forty minutes on foot from Yoki's house to hers. This was a week ago, before I got my license. I could have told Yoki I needed a ride to her place. I could have phoned and invited her to come over on her motorcycle. But I wanted to go see her under my own power, so she'd realize I was serious. Also, I didn't want Yoki teasing me.

It was around five when we finished work and got back to Yoki's place. The sun sets early in the mountains, so it was already turning dark. We always eat supper at six thirty. I told Yoki I'd be back by then and set out, pretending to go for a walk. I crossed the little bridge and headed downhill by the Kamusari River. I knew Yoki was watching me with suspicion, but I didn't look back.

Along the way to Naka district, where Nao lives, there are no houses. On my right was the gurgling river, and close at hand on my left was the mountainside, with a cypress canopy overhead. I was freaked out, to tell the truth. Nobody in Kamusari ever goes out walking after dark. Hardly any cars go by (nobody but a local would have business on a road that deep in the mountains), and with no streetlights, it's pitch-dark. At any moment, a wild boar might come charging at me, or I might miss my footing and land in the river. I walked fast, fearful of the surprisingly dense blackness.

Since the trip is forty minutes each way, to get back in time for supper I could spend only ten minutes with Nao, assuming I'd be able to see her at all. Even so, I stubbornly kept going. In the back of my mind, I hoped that when she saw I'd walked all the way to see her, she'd take me a little more seriously.

In my defense, going to driving school had taken up so much of my time that I hadn't seen Nao in quite a while. I'd applied to the school in mid-June. During the rainy season, we often have time off, so Seiichi suggested that I take the opportunity to get my driver's license. Tuition costs a bundle, but I had nearly enough saved up to cover it. Saving money is easy here. Yoki provides me with room and board (I make a minimum contribution for meals), and there's no place in the village to spend money on clothes. Nakamura Lumber supplies my work clothes free of charge, along with tools. So I followed Seiichi's suggestion and enrolled in the school, paying mostly out of my savings and making up the difference by a small advance on my salary.

The problem was how to get to and from the school. Kamusari is an hour by car from the last station on the local line. The school's courtesy bus doesn't come anywhere near the village. As I was racking my brain over this seemingly insoluble problem, Miho volunteered to drive me: "I'll be going shopping in Hisai anyway, so I might as well give you a lift." She has a red compact car that she parks on the assembly hall grounds.

And so I started at the driving school in Hisai, riding there and back with Miho—nearly an hour each way. It wasn't easy juggling things; I had all my regular work to do, and I couldn't always reserve a session when I wanted to. Still, I managed to get my learner's permit with no trouble. By then it was summertime and we were super-busy at work, so I had to take a long break.

I never used to like school or studying, but driving school was really fun. Sure, some of the instructors were hard-asses, but in the car Miho and I talked and sang, so I could let off steam. I helped with the grocery shopping, too, picking out food, bagging up everything, and carrying the groceries to the car for her. While I was in school, she would go to the public library and read a book or have a cup of coffee somewhere.

In the fall when we weren't so busy, I picked up my lessons again. We started on-the-road practice, which I found pretty nerve-racking and exhausting. On top of my regular work in the forests, I had to study for the final exam, too. With so much going on, there was no time to see Nao.

I couldn't go on that way. I had to do something. Not that Nao and I are in a relationship. She knows how I feel about her, but she's hesitant about making a commitment. The problem is, she's only got eyes for Seiichi—her sister Risa's husband. That's right, an illicit love. But I have a feeling that isn't the only reason. She doesn't have much faith in me. *There aren't any other girls his age in the village; that's why he fell for me, because I'm the only one around. And anyway, one of these days he'll give up on forestry and go back to the city where he came from.* That's what she thinks.

That suspicious nature of hers is something else I really like about her, by the way.

I can't wave a wand and banish her suspicions. I can't argue against the idea that I like her only because there aren't any other girls here to choose from. If I'd met her in the city, where there are tons of girls, I might not have fallen for her so hard. But I'm sure she would have stood out to me. Since falling in love with her, I haven't ever compared her to anyone else, so it's hard to say.

And whether I will someday, for some reason, give up on forestry and head back to Yokohama, or whether I'll stay here permanently and make forestry my life's work, I don't know. Only the gods of Kamusari know that for sure. All I can say is, I want to live here and work here for as long as I possibly can.

Anyway, I have no proof of my love and I can't make her any promises, but the least I can do is go see her whenever I have the chance, right? Otherwise she'll only be even more mistrustful and never open up to me.

And so I started on that long walk so I could see Nao and tell her I was about to get my license. But really I was going because not seeing her for so long was driving me crazy.

A road in the dark feels longer than it actually is. There were no turnoffs on the way, but my heart started beating faster as I worried that maybe somehow I'd gotten off onto a side road and was wandering, lost, in the mountains. I breathed a huge sigh of relief when I finally came to the intersection with Ise Road (though at night that road is frequented mainly by wild raccoon dogs) and saw the lights of Naka district ahead.

Nao's house is next to a big shrine. She fixed up her grandparents' old house and lives there alone. She teaches second grade in the local school. I was pretty sure she'd be home by then, and just as I expected, her big Kawasaki motorcycle was there. I saw it out of the corner of my eye as I went up the stone steps and stood before her door to collect myself.

"Anybody home?" I called out, opening the door. (Nobody locks their door here.) The interior was dark and silent.

This was a scenario I hadn't counted on. Disappointed, I closed the door and leaned against the outside wall. Moonlight shone on the treetops. Was I going to have to turn around and make the long trek back without having seen Nao at all?

The sound of an engine came closer, and a car pulled up in front of the house. Was she back from a trip to the store? But she owned only a motorcycle.

I stood up straight and peered down from the top of the steps, just in time to see her emerge from the passenger seat of a white sedan (I don't pay much attention to names of cars).

"Thank you very much." Nao bowed politely in the driver's direction. From what I could make out of the silhouette inside the car, the driver was male. An emergency buzzer went off in my head. I craned my neck, trying to see who it was. Damn, the moon wasn't bright enough. It was too dark to see much, but I had the impression of someone in his late twenties.

The guy executed a neat three-point turn. (I was still counting poles at the driving school, trying to master parallel parking.) He opened his window and beckoned to Nao, who was standing there to see him off. She immediately walked up to the car and bent down a little. He looked up at her and said something. She laughed. If he had kissed her, I was ready to grab a kitchen knife and commit *seppuku* on the spot.

I craned my neck farther and farther, and the silent pressure I was exerting from the shadows seemed to do the trick. He finally gave his horn a tap in farewell and drove off. *Don't you know it's nighttime, moron? Quit trying to be cute and butt outa here.* Yoki's crassness might have rubbed off on me.

Nao was bowing in the direction of the departing car. Then all of a sudden, she turned toward the house and started coming up the steps. When she saw me she gave a little scream of surprise, and that startled me so much, I bet I jumped a foot in the air.

"It's you!" She covered her chest with both hands. "What are you doing here? You nearly gave me a heart attack."

I bridled. "What do you mean, what am I doing here?"

A window opened next door, and the voice of a middle-aged woman called with concern, "Nao dear, is something wrong? I thought I heard you scream just now."

"It's nothing. Sorry."

"As long as you're all right. Good night, dear."

"Good night."

Nao grabbed me by the arm and pulled me over in front of the door, out of the neighbor's sight. Apparently the neighborhood crime watch was on the alert. Jeez, can't a guy even call on a girl he likes without setting off alarms?

"If you're not a stalker, would you mind not waiting in ambush for me? You took a few years off my life."

"It's not an ambush. I came to see you and you were out, that's all."

She opened the door. "Did you have some kind of business with me?" She sounded puzzled.

What, I can't come over unless I've got business with you? I started to say, and stopped myself. We weren't in a relationship, after all. But I was angry and hurt, and so I lashed out again, even more harshly than before. "I've told you how I feel about you, and all you do is put me off! Who was that guy just now?"

"I'm not putting you off."

"No? Then you'll be my girl? Or maybe you already are—we're together and I just didn't know it?" *Whoa, slow down.* I knew better than to push her like that, but the words came out.

One hand on the door, her body half turned, she looked down with a troubled expression. I let out a long breath. She was trembling slightly, so I stepped back to give her some space.

"Sorry," I said. "I wanted to tell you I've been going to driving school, and I'm just about to get my license."

"Oh, yeah? That's nice." She finally raised her head, and the moon lit her cheek. She looked really pretty.

"I just wanted you to know." Reluctantly, I took another step back. "I'll be off, then."

"How'd you get here? Aren't you with Yoki?"

"No, I walked."

"You *walked*?" She sounded genuinely astonished. "Just to tell me you were about to get your license?"

It was my turn to marvel at how slow on the uptake she was. She was pretty, and her students all loved her, but when it came to romance, she was tone-deaf.

I drew closer to her again, taking back the space I had relinquished, and placed both hands on the door, one on either side of her face. My body blocked the moonlight, putting her face in shadow. I whispered, "You want me to say it? Shall I tell you why I walked all the way here?"

She looked up at me and . . . burst out laughing. "Sorry. You don't have to say it. I get it." She bent over, laughing hard now. "You wanted to see me, right?"

30

Did she have to be so unfeeling about it? The moment was gone, wrecked. I felt a wave of red-hot embarrassment and let my arms drop limply to my sides. "Right," I said sullenly.

Wiping away tears of laughter, she said, "That guy just now is a colleague of mine. There was a teacher training session today at Kawanaka Elementary School, so we both went, and he gave me a ride home, that's all."

"You sure seemed to be on good terms with him."

"What, are you jealous?"

"Yes."

"Well, when you get your license, take me for a spin."

This lifted my spirits, but somehow I didn't want her to see through me, so I kept on scowling. "I haven't got a cool-looking car like his."

And that's when she said it.

"You're *small*, you know that? A little jealousy can be endearing, but self-pity, never. All a car needs to do is run, if you ask me." She slipped inside the house, leaving me standing there. "You'd better be getting back, then. Good night."

The door closed. I was dismissed. For the next forty minutes I trudged back home, the word "small" going round and round in my head. As I reflected on the smallness and ugliness of how I had spoken and behaved, shame turned my face as red as the lanterns outside a bar and propelled me up the steep, dark road.

After quarreling with Nao (or rather, after she one-sidedly called me "small"), I lost heart. Yoki, Miho, and Granny Shige immediately picked up on the change. Even Noko could tell something was off; when I got home late for supper, after seven o'clock, he came up to me and sniffed my feet with concern.

I'd gone to see Nao straight from work, without taking a bath or changing my clothes. I wonder if she thought I stank. I hope not.

"That was some walk." Yoki was sitting in the entryway, clipping his toenails. "We went ahead and ate without you."

"Sure. I'm sorry I was late."

Yoki looked up in surprise at my tone. "What's goin' on? You look washed out."

"I'm fine." To avoid his eyes, I headed for the kitchen.

Miho followed me. "Go sit down, Yuki. I'll heat up some supper for you right away. Yoki, when you finish there, heat up the bath, will you?"

"Yes, ma'am." He stood up and went out the back door to get firewood to heat the old-fashioned bath.

I felt bad about Miho waiting on me like that, but I did as she said and went to sit down in the family room. Granny Shige was sitting at the low, round table with a teacup in her hand. She looked at me hard enough to bore a hole in me—I'd heard that expression before, and now I knew exactly what it meant.

Finally, unable to bear it anymore, I turned toward her awkwardly. "What is it, Granny Shige?"

"Nothin'." She smiled her toothless smile. All the while I ate the food Miho brought, she kept smiling complacently to herself. It was enough to drive a man crazy. Seriously.

The next day, I left work early, just after lunch. At the foot of the mountain, Miho was waiting in her little red car. "Hi, Yuki," she said.

"Thanks for coming to pick me up. I appreciate it." She was going to give me a ride to the driving school and do her grocery shopping in Hisai.

She gave the steering wheel a turn and started down the gravel road. Forest roads are hard on compact cars; there's a lot of bouncing. The gravel spray seemed targeted right at my butt. We rode along for a while in silence, half-afraid that if we opened our mouths, we might bite our tongues. When we finally came to a paved road, she spoke up.

"Today's your final exam, right? Are you nervous?"

"Not really."

"You've passed every test with flying colors, haven't you?"

"Yes. I'm paying with an advance from Seiichi, so the more do-overs I have, the more salary I lose."

"I'm impressed. The first time I took the test for my learner's permit, I failed, and I couldn't always earn stickers for my driving skills in class, either. I had to pay for an extra three sessions."

Despite this disclaimer, her driving was really smooth. She went easy on the brakes and took curves with caution. She was safe and steady behind the wheel—not at all what you'd expect from a demon of jealousy.

"Say, Yuki. Yesterday you went to see Nao, right?"

"The secret's out, I guess."

"Oh, we all knew. Last night Yoki was worried that maybe she gave you the boot. I'm supposed to ask you casually what happened."

So Yoki was worried about me. Now that I thought of it, at work that morning he'd treated me with such awkward consideration, it had felt weird. Remembering, I laughed. "We kind of quarreled. I acted immature, pushing her and making a fool of myself, and she got fed up."

"Don't be discouraged." She sounded amused. "Nao's a sweet kid, but she's got a wicked tongue. Don't give up. All you have to do is hang on and not let go."

"Really?"

"Really. Women all know that men never really grow up. If we let that get to us all the time, we could never have a relationship."

Spoken by Miho, who was married to Yoki, this argument was persuasive.

The little red car wound down the twisting mountain road between forests rising on either side. As we left Kamusari behind, the river widened, flanked now by rice paddies reduced to stubble after harvest. At the first red light we came to (there are no traffic lights in Kamusari), I looked out my window at sparrows scattered around the brown paddies.

I felt I needed the perspective of someone with experience, so I decided to go ahead and ask her.

"You and Yoki have known each other since you were children. Did you have any doubts about dating him and marrying him?"

"No, I can't say I did."

"But he's pretty crazy."

"I know it." She smiled. "But I could never have loved anybody else, so what choice did I have?"

I stole a look at her. The light turned green, and she exerted gentle pressure on the accelerator.

Yoki was her first and only love; she'd had eyes only for him, and she'd married him. He meant everything to her. His fooling around with other women would, of course, make her insanely jealous.

"Would you like to hear how we fell in love?" she asked a bit shyly.

Clearly she wanted to tell me, so I said, "Yes, I would."

Hands firmly on the steering wheel, she squirmed in her seat and then sat up straight. "I always loved Yoki, and everybody in Kamusari knows it, for sure. I've never come right out and told our story to anybody. I'm not sure I even can. Hoo boy."

Even though she was the one who brought it up, she sounded embarrassed.

"Go ahead and tell me," I said. "You can do it."

And with that bit of encouragement, she began: Yoki had always lived around the corner, and as far back as she could remember, she'd always had a crush on him.

The end. Well, that didn't take long, I thought with irony. She went on.

"I lived with my folks at the foot of the bridge and helped run the store." (That's the Nakamuraya, the lone store in Kamusari district.) "Yoki used to come by a lot. When he was little, he'd come with his folks, hand in hand."

"They died young, didn't they?" I interjected. As I spoke, I realized I'd never met Seiichi's parents, either. It struck me as strange. Yoki's and

Seiichi's parents must have been about the same age as Miho's. A little older than Iwao. There weren't many people of that generation in the village.

"Yeah." Miho looked a bit subdued. "Yoki doesn't talk much about them. What happened was so painful. I'm sure eventually you'll find out all about it."

In other words, leave it alone for now. I got the message and didn't press the point.

"When Yoki came by the store"—her voice was cheerful again— "he'd cram candy in his mouth when my mom wasn't looking, and lift up my skirt."

"That's awful."

"Yes, but he was nice to me, too. When other boys teased me, he'd beat them up, and sometimes he'd bring me flowers he'd picked or a crawdad he'd caught."

He sounded like a child of nature. And he'd won Miho's admiration without spending a dime, I noted.

They both attended Kamusari Elementary, two grades apart. "Even back then, kids were few and far between in Kamusari district. Yoki was a playmate and a big brother to me, too. Though of course I always saw him as more than that."

"What about Seiichi?"

"Well, he was older, and of course when he grew up he was destined to be the master, wasn't he? It was like he lived in another world."

That's the way it goes. Seiichi was more polished than Yoki. He had more brains, more common sense, more kindness, too. Plus, his family was rich. But Miho was drawn to wildness—to a guy who seemed perfectly capable of strangling a wild boar with his bare hands or chowing down hungrily on weeds. There's no accounting for taste, I mused, listening to her go on.

"All through elementary school and junior high, Yoki was really popular with girls. I told him I liked him, but he just laughed."

35

Did most girls go for the wild type, then? I was starting to lose confidence. Meanwhile, Miho's inner demon of jealousy was rearing its head.

"He lost his virginity to a divorcée living in Shimo district. She was thirty if she was a day. Pretty in a way, and sexy, but what kind of woman invites a junior-high-school boy into her house?"

"It's criminal."

"You bet it is! And Yoki, the dummy, fell for it." Steering expertly, Miho speeded up and zoomed past a truck.

For the love of God, woman, stay calm . . .

"But you know what? I never gave up. When Yoki went to high school in Matsusaka, I followed him."

"So you both went to the same high school, too?"

"Oh, no. Yoki's school was crawling with *yanki* types—always in and out of trouble. My grades were good. I got into Matsusaka High." She sounded proud.

My own high school was a lot more like Yoki's than I cared to admit, so I squirmed a bit.

After going on to say she'd graduated from college and then worked in Tsu, Miho went back to Yoki's—and her—high school days. "Yoki had no end of girlfriends in high school, too. Every time I saw him, he was with somebody different. I'd wait for him by the school gate, and when he saw me, he'd do a double take."

"You were stalking him!" I was indignant, my own stalker tendencies forgotten.

"No, silly, I was in love. If I hadn't done that much, he'd have forgotten all about me."

I doubted that. Despite their quarrels, Yoki seemed to me to always be looking out for Miho. Or was he scared of rousing her jealousy?

Her ever-growing love for Yoki had frightened her with its intensity, Miho said. She decided she ought to turn her attention on other men for once in her life, and for a while she dated a classmate. "But it was no good. Kissing was all right, but I couldn't go beyond that. All I could think was how much more fun it would be if I were with Yoki."

"When I'm with Yoki at work, my nerves get frayed and that's all."

"That's because you're a man. Yoki's a master at showing a woman a good time."

Whoa. Did she mean between the sheets? I stole a look at her.

"Idiot. I meant in general."

After high school, Yoki went back to Kamusari and joined Nakamura Lumber. From then on, he and Seiichi had been traipsing around from mountain to mountain.

"After Yoki left Matsusaka, I panicked. I knew that once he was back in the village, he'd be an eligible bachelor. Girls would be making eyes at him right and left. I was terrified he might marry one of them."

"Seems to me he's more the type that would enjoy staying a bachelor."

"There's where you're wrong, Yuki. At heart he's a homebody. He wanted nothing more than to marry some girl and have a peaceful home life—while going on doing as he pleased on the side."

"That's rotten."

"Yeah." She looked a bit sad. "But that's his nature. He needs companionship."

"You're not just 'some girl' to him," I said hastily, to cheer her. "And lately, I swear, he hasn't been fooling around at all."

Her face brightened. "That's right, he hasn't. It's all your doing, Yuki. Thank goodness you came to Kamusari. I do think nobody could make him a better wife than me. Nobody knows better than me about his personality, his thinking, and all he's been through. The only trouble is"—she sighed—"we've been married for quite a while now, and we have no kids. I feel bad I haven't been able to give him that."

She wanted children? I hadn't expected to hear this. I felt unsettled. "You shouldn't feel that way," I said. "I've never once heard Yoki say he wants a family, and anyway, you might still have kids."

"True. For a while we went to a fertility clinic. But it was too far, and the treatments were painful. Yoki put his foot down. 'Don't do it,' he said. 'We'll have ourselves a baby when the time comes. All I ever need is you.'"

This surprised me. Yoki really came out with a smooth line like that? Alone with Miho, he was surprisingly straightforward in his expression of affection. Maybe his showering her with affection that way in the daytime accounted for the frequent sounds of lovemaking coming from their room at night. Embarrassed, I scratched my cheek.

"You still haven't told me how the two of you got together."

"Oh, right." She turned pink. "It started at the cherry-blossom-viewing party."

On top of the little mountain behind Seiichi's house is a magnificent tree called the Kamusari Cherry Tree. Every year, the villagers have a big party underneath its branches. I've been to the party, and there's plenty of drinking and singing—it gets really lively.

Miho's comment reminded me of something Iwao once said about the party: "Yoki shoved Miho down in the bushes." I think it was when Yoki was still in high school. Or maybe he'd just graduated? Miho would have been a high schooler, too. *That's against the law, Yoki!* Surely that wasn't the start of their romance?

But it was. Miho said, "After the cherry-blossom-viewing party, it was a done deal. First, I threw myself at him. 'Take me,' I said. 'Now or never. Make up your mind, right now!'"

What a couple! A pair of fastball pitchers. As near as I could piece it together, here's what happened.

At the party, Yoki went up to Miho, who was then in high school, to talk to her. She'd come home that weekend for the occasion.

"I hear some bean sprout at Matsusaka High is your boyfriend now. Just because I've come back to the village and can't keep an eye on you, and your parents aren't around either, don't go do anything wild."

"None of your business. And who told you I have a boyfriend?"

"I've got my sources in Matsusaka. I know what's going on. Just don't do anything to give your folks grief."

"Unlike you, I lead a pure life, thank you very much. And the fastest way for you to ease my parents' mind about me would be to marry me."

"There you go again."

"What's wrong? Don't you like me?"

"I like you fine. But I've known you my whole life. After all this time, I can't look at you that way."

"Then leave me be. I've told you time and again, you're the only one for me. But if you won't have me, fine. I'll go back to Matsusaka and sleep around with all kinds of men."

"Why would you do that?"

"I don't want to die a virgin."

"Don't be a dope. Who says you hafta sleep with all kinds of men? Be reasonable. Sleep with just one guy, someone you like."

"You're the only one for me, and I don't want anyone else falling for me, either. So when I feel like sleeping with someone, I'll do it with . . . whoever."

"Talk sense, will you?"

"In the end I'll probably fall in with yakuza and get sold into sexual slavery."

"Fat chance."

"That's what you think. It's bound to happen. Look, I don't care if all you see when you look at me is a childhood friend. If you have any thought of saving me from a life of degradation, then make up your mind. Take me or leave me, right here, right now!"

What a woman. Listening, I couldn't help laughing. "That's intimidation!"

"Maybe."

"So he took you?"

"He probably thought if we had sex once, I'd be satisfied. Whereas if I kept mooning over him, I might never find someone else."

"And that was the start of your relationship."

"Um, no. Actually, after that he avoided me. Gave me the cold shoulder when I came home on vacation. It hurt."

We had now entered Hisai. The driving school was straight ahead.

"Tell me something, Yuki," she said, as if a thought had just struck her. "You think some people are content to have sex just once? I can see doing without it completely. But if you slept with someone you really, really liked, wouldn't you naturally want to do it again? Isn't that just human nature?"

I folded my arms and thought. "Let me see. I've never really heard of someone having sex just once. Once you break that barrier, the hurdle gets lower."

My words filled me with sudden alarm. "Wait a minute! Are you saying that after one time with Yoki, the hurdle was lowered, and you really did start sleeping with whoever?"

She laughed. "I'm not saying."

She pulled up in front of the driving school. "I'll tell you the rest on the way back. Good luck on your final exam."

What! You can't leave it hanging there! How'm I supposed to concentrate on my test?

Fortunately, my driving skills were solid, and even with my worries about Miho in the back of my mind, I passed the road test on my first try. When she came to pick me up, I smiled and waved.

"You passed? Congratulations!"

"Thank you. I still have to take the paper test, though."

"I'll drive you. No problem. Is next weekend okay?" She seemed genuinely excited by my success. "I was so sure you'd pass, I bought sea bream *and* beef for supper."

"Wow, thank you." I had other things on my mind besides that night's menu. "Getting back to your story . . ."

"Oh, that." She nodded. "You can relax. All the time I was in college, and even after that when I was working in Tsu, I didn't have a boyfriend. Compared to Yoki, other men were bland and boring."

"So you came close to going your whole life having had sex just that one time."

"Yes. But Yoki didn't let that happen. Thank goodness." Miho looked up through the windshield at the evening sky. Her mind seemed far away.

Eyes on the road, please!

"After I'd been living in Tsu about three years, one day, all of a sudden, he showed up at my apartment."

"Out of the blue? Did you let him in?" The guy had real nerve.

"I was still in love with him. Of course I did." She made tea, she said.

Yoki took a sip. "So how's it goin'? You figured out yet I'm not the only good-lookin' guy in the world?"

"No. All I know is you're the only one for me."

Seated across from Miho at the table, Yoki looked at her silently. Then he set his teacup down, took hers out of her hand, and set it down, too. (He *definitely* had nerve.) He stood up, grabbed her by the arm, and pulled her to the bed.

Then, Miho told me, Yoki said, "I give up. If you haven't changed your tune after all this time, you must be right. From now on, you'll be the only one for me, too." She looked at me. "And that's how Yoki and I came to be married."

"But even after he got married, there *were* others . . ." I murmured aloud without thinking.

"I know!" Her hair practically stood on end. "That no-good so-and-so. He makes me sooo mad."

I'd awakened the demon of jealousy. Hastily I said, "I'm sorry, Miho, I shouldn't have said that. There's no one but you in his life now. Really."

She calmed down, and the danger of a collision or the car spinning out of control was averted. I realized I'd better hurry up and get my license so I could drive myself, or no telling what might happen.

Since we'd left Hisai and headed uphill alongside the Kamusari River, the sky had darkened considerably, and fewer and fewer cars were on the road. Now, in place of red taillights, ahead was a smattering of stars.

"Now how come I told you all that about Yoki and me?" Miho cocked her head, puzzled.

You're the one who brought it up, not me. I was silent.

"I know! It's because you and Nao quarreled." Suddenly the conversation catapulted backward.

"Not really . . ."

"When you get your license, ask her out for a drive. You can borrow Yoki's pickup or my car, either one, any time."

"Would she come, though?"

"Don't worry. Learn from my experience. It pays to be bold."

"Okay, here's what I learned. Your story boils down to this: you and Yoki have cared deeply for each other for a really long time."

"Smarty-pants!" She laughed, tickled. She really was a woman of charm, brimming with vitality. No wonder Yoki thought the world of her and had made an unconditional surrender.

Even after she met other people and took her time thinking it over, Miho's feelings had never wavered. Her attraction to Yoki wasn't a mistake, nor was it just because they lived in an underpopulated village. Against all odds, Miho had encountered the one man for her in a Kamusari village in decline. Her man of destiny. And through sheer force of will, she had made him see that she was his destiny, too.

Is that kind of thinking girlish, sentimental? In any case, I'm not giving up. I'm going to ask Nao to come on a drive with me. And this time I'll come right out and say it: *You're the only one for me.*

I've got no car, no money, and no fancy job. I work in forestry—the kind of job where, overnight, a typhoon can destroy thousands of trees and wipe out a century or more of hard work. It's a huge gamble. Plus the work is dangerous and demanding. But it's also hugely rewarding. My work is valuable and important—no less so than teaching school.

Nao knows all that. I had no reason to feel inferior to the guy dropping her off.

Miho's jealousy had quieted down. The little red car ran smoothly up into the mountains, drawing closer and closer to Kamusari. The dark silhouette of the mountains was rimmed with silver stars. I would borrow Yoki's pickup and invite Nao on a drive. I would save up my money and buy my own truck. I would let Nao know I meant business, in no uncertain terms. Once I had all that settled in my mind, I was so excited I had to come up and write about it.

Okay, everybody, wish me luck! I'll let you know next time whether or not Nao said yes.

3

THE THIRD NIGHT

THE MASTER OF KAMUSARI

Yuki Hirano, at your service again! Greetings, or as we say in Kamusari, naa-naa.

The cold set in early this year. The nightly racket of insects sounding off like a noisy band has fallen silent. The closer it is to winter, the quieter the village becomes, until finally it's wrapped entirely in snow.

It's November now, and trees on the mountaintops have started changing color. Of course, most of the mountains around the village are planted with cedar and/or cypress, so they stay green all fall and winter. But it's not the soft, translucent green of early spring or the heavy, deep green of summer. It's more subdued, a dark, mossy green, as the trees ready themselves for winter under thick, white, overhanging clouds. Here and there, starting at the top of the mountain, mixed in with the evergreens, foliage on the few remaining deciduous trees slowly turns red and gold.

You may wonder why any deciduous trees would be left on mountainsides planted with conifers. There are several reasons.

First, they serve to mark boundaries. Not every mountain has a single owner. Seiichi owns a hundred or more mountains, but most owners only have title to part of one. The east side might belong to A and the west to B, for example. You can't build walls or string up rope to mark off the border, so instead they plant deciduous trees. Then everyone understands that all the cedars and cypresses east of a certain zelkova, say, belong to A, and those to the west belong to B. Where a sign or placard would only rust or rot away, a tree native to the mountain will live for a century or more. And believe me, one deciduous tree among row upon row of conifers really stands out. It makes a natural dividing line.

Second, the terrain might not be suitable for planting trees. Mountain slopes aren't even. They have rough spots, and sometimes there's a deep cavity where a landslide occurred. There can be huge boulders, too. All of that makes it hard to plant cypresses and cedars. (Although Yoki has the strength of an ox—I can picture him moving boulders with his bare hands.) The locals take a relaxed, naa-naa approach to life, so when it looks like a stretch of land would be hard to plant, they'll take one look and agree, "Let's not." On the other hand, sometimes even when a mountainside is so steep it's more like a cliff, they'll go right ahead and plant saplings. Especially Yoki. Besides being as strong as an ox, he's fearless. I've seen him shoulder a basketful of saplings and plant them all the way down a cliffside so steep that I'd wet my pants if I tried it. But not everybody has his monkey-like dexterity, so deciduous trees are allowed to grow in places where tree planting is impossible, giving us the welcome view of colorful leaves in the fall.

Third, it could be that the owner gave up forestry. Seiichi is troubled by the way foreign lumber floods the market in Japan, crowding out the domestic industry. Forestry is hardly an efficient way to make a living, so a lot of landowners don't even try. If the land they own has been planted with cypress or cedar, then to maintain the quality of the forest, Nakamura Lumber or the local union will look after it on their behalf.

But often, once the timber has been felled and shipped out, the owner says, "Don't bother replanting. Forestry doesn't pay enough. I'm quitting the business." Then there'll be a gap on the mountainside. Ferns move in, birds and breezes carry in seeds, and trees start to grow. In time, there'll be a deciduous forest. Or sometimes an excess of ferns prevents trees from taking root and growing, or bamboo takes over, spreading with great vitality. Then Seiichi might negotiate with the owner to buy the land, or he'll look after it at a special discount rate. There's not much profit in it, but little by little we'll cut back the ferns and bamboo so trees can grow. Without enough trees, either deciduous or conifer, there's a high risk of landslide. Birds and beasts have fewer places of rest, too, and the mountain ceases to store water.

And so a mountain planted with conifers will often have one area devoted to deciduous trees. But there's a fourth reason: sometimes a deciduous tree is just impossible to chop down. Before planting a tract of land with conifers, we clear out all the deciduous trees, but as Iwao says, "Sometimes a tree is so sublime, felling it would be a desecration."

I have yet to come across a stand of immense, ancient trees in the course of my work. Forestry has been going on around Kamusari since the Tokugawa period, going back more than five centuries, so there are no old-growth deciduous forests. Even so, here and there we'll come across a huge camphor tree or a zelkova that does seem somehow holy, standing proud amid the evergreens. When they come across a tree like that, Iwao and Old Man Saburo always offer tea or water from their canteens and then stand before it quietly with their palms pressed together. It seems less an expression of faith than a perfectly natural way to greet a superior.

On the mountains, we have no one to rely on but ourselves. There's always the risk of an accident or a sudden, dangerous change in the weather. Under those conditions, I guess revering the god of the mountain or the god of an enormous tree comes naturally. People pray only in times of trouble, they say, which to me seems like a suspect use of religion—but the point is, this line of work is inherently so demanding and dangerous that all anybody can do is trust their luck and leave their fate in the hands of the gods.

One day we were lopping branches on West Mountain, and at lunchtime Iwao told a story about trying to chop down a huge zelkova on South Mountain ages ago, in his twenties. "The site had been neglected so long, it was a deciduous forest. Before we could plant our cedar saplings, we went around chopping it all down, chestnut trees, maples, you name it. Then we came to the zelkova." It was magnificent, he said, with a trunk as big around as the arm spans of three men. "Back when that site was originally planted, they must have left it there to mark the border. It grew and grew, till it was a giant."

"Our team leader then was a fellow named Sugishita," interjected Old Man Saburo. "He's long gone now, but he was a good worker and devout, too."

"That he was." Iwao nodded. "When he got mad, he'd come at you with his fist, so that's what we called him—Fist."

Like calling your dog "Dog." Must have been a hot-blooded guy like Yoki. Lucky thing our leader's Seiichi—he'd never resort to his fists. Maybe I'll start calling Yoki "Fist" for fun.

Iwao had been young, Old Man Saburo in middle age. They'd stood there, raring to go, excited by the challenge of felling a tree so massive. But not Fist. He calmed them down, and after pouring water at the base of the zelkova, he crouched down and pressed his palms together. Then he stood up and walked around the tree three times, head down, as if he were listening to the rustling of the leaves. Finally, he stopped in front of Iwao and Old Man Saburo, who were waiting impatiently, and made a pronouncement:

"This tree has been protecting this slope for generations. It's provided a dwelling place for the god of the mountain and sheltered other trees and animals from storms and snow, saving lives. I'm against cutting it down."

Iwao chuckled. "To be honest, my first thought was, *What kind of airy-fairy talk is this?* Old Man Saburo scoffed right along with me. 'Don't be ridiculous,' we said. 'We can't do our job if you go on like that. If you don't want to be involved, fine. Stand back, and we'll cut it down while you watch.'"

They picked up their brand-new chain saws (this all happened when lightweight chain saws were just coming into wide use) and marched toward the zelkova, fired up to get the job done.

"And then a funny thing happened," said Old Man Saburo, cocking his head. "All of a sudden my bowels went loose. I squatted down in the brush and couldn't move. Hurt like the dickens."

"When I saw that, I felt a chill," said Iwao. "Fist just laughed: 'What'd I tell you!' Yes, sir, we gave up trying to cut that tree down. We all stood in front of it and bowed our heads. And just like that, Old Man Saburo's stomachache vanished." Ever since, they said, that zelkova has been worshiped as a *shimboku*, a divine tree.

I was impressed—not just by the tree but by Saburo's stomachache giving birth to a legend. "The world's a mysterious place, all right," I said, and bit into one of Miho's supersized onigiri. I didn't believe in the curse of the zelkova, but the man who'd gotten the stomachache was sitting right next to me. I had to accept that part as true.

"That zelkova is still there on South Mountain," Seiichi added. "You'll be going there off and on for work, Yuki. Be sure to stop by, make an offering, and pay your respects."

"Okay." I nodded.

Noko was snuffling around the roots of a forty-year-old cypress.

"It's amazing to think you could start to cut down a big tree and get struck sick that way," I said. "Makes tree cutting kind of scary."

"Not a bit," said Yoki, lying on his back. "You treat trees with the respect they deserve, but when the time comes to cut one down, you do. If something feels off, all you gotta do is step back."

"You've cut down your share of big trees, too, haven't you, Yoki?" I said. "Has anything like what happened to Old Man Saburo ever happened to you?"

"Let me think." He rubbed the tip of his nose. "Nope. I only got sick on the mountain one time."

"That was heatstroke, Yoki, pure and simple," said Seiichi with a half smile. He turned to me to explain. "In the middle of summer, we were cutting underbrush. Lunchtime came, and no Yoki, so I went to look for him. I found him collapsed in a clump of grass. He was bright red."

"I didn't know what hit me." Yoki sat up and patted Noko on the head. "They didn't publish warnings about heatstroke on TV and in the paper then, the way they do now. I was hard at work, clearing brush and weeds, and all at once I felt dizzy. I remember thinking, *Maybe it's an earthquake.* Next thing I knew, I was flat on my back, looking up at blue sky."

"And then Seiichi came to get you?"

"Not right away. I picked myself up, wondering what had happened, and lit a cigarette to steady my nerves."

"Ooh. Bad idea?"

"You bet it was. One puff and I was woozy, then out like a light. Blacked out again. This time when I came to, Seiichi was beside me, stomping on the grass. My cigarette had fallen and set it smoldering."

"He gave me a real scare." Seiichi let out a long breath. "I always used to say, 'Be extra careful when you smoke on the mountains.' He easily could have started a forest fire. From then on, I made it a rule: no smoking on the mountains, period."

Yoki looked dissatisfied. "Yeah, but man—talk about heartless! The whole time you were putting out the fire, you never even looked at me, lying there helpless. I mean, it wasn't even a real fire—some weeds got a tiny bit scorched, that's all. Seems to me you coulda said something

50

to your best friend—*How ya doin', buddy, you okay?* Was that too much to ask?"

"I kept the fire from spreading to you. You should be thanking me, not complaining."

Seiichi and Yoki have completely different personalities and ways of thinking. Yoki's got a reckless streak. He can't sit still. After work we go back home together, and he'll be out in the entryway, sharpening his ax, while I'm in the kitchen helping Miho get supper on. Sounds peaceful, right? But by the time I turn to call, "Supper's ready," he's gone. While my back's turned, he'll sneak out of the house, climb in his pickup, and take off to go drinking in town.

Miho fumes, Granny Shige starts praying, and I pace around; Yoki comes home in the middle of the night in high spirits, having hired someone to drive him. Sometimes the proxy driver arrives alone and tells us, "The mister jumped out a ways back."

Then Miho's anger boils over and she can't sleep. Granny Shige raises her eyes to heaven and says, "That boy'll be the death of me."

It's up to me to go out and look for him. If he jumped out close to town I wouldn't bother, but usually I find him asleep somewhere nearby, on the riverbank. Why he chooses there to conk out when he's drunk, you'd have to ask him. I've got no idea.

"The closer he gets to home, the more he can't stand the thought of seeing my face, so he tries to escape." Miho's fury is powerful enough to lift Mt. Kamusari a foot higher.

"I think you have it backward," I tell her. "When he sees he's close to home, he feels so safe and secure that he gets ahead of himself and jumps out."

I'll find him lying sprawled by the river on grasses wet with dew, a stone for his pillow, snoring away. In the summertime, he gets covered in mosquito bites. In the wintertime, an ordinary person would freeze to death. But there's nothing ordinary about Yoki; he lies there sound asleep, smiling. I'm stuck with the unhappy task of hoisting him on my back and carrying him home in the dead of night. For some reason, on those nights the sky is always filled with a profusion of stars, as if they're watching over him as he sleeps.

Unlike Yoki, who doesn't give a hoot about either keeping up appearances or preserving peace at home, Seiichi is sensible and reliable. As the master, he's in a position of leadership in the village, and he keeps Nakamura Lumber running smoothly. His family life is on track, too; Risa and Santa have complete faith in him. When he drives to Nagoya on business, the two of them stand and wave until they can't see his taillights anymore. If it were Yoki, Miho would be full of dark suspicion: "Business, huh? Just make sure you're not off to see some woman." The bento lunches Risa packs for Seiichi to eat on the mountain are something else, too: colorful and elaborate. They look amazing.

Seiichi rarely talks about his family, but it's easy to tell how much they mean to him. Sometimes in his spare moments at work he'll pick up a couple of acorns and polish them, or gather akebia, a fruit-like wild banana. Once I saw him come across a gorgeous pheasant feather and stick it in his back pocket. They must have been presents for Risa and Santa. I can imagine the three of them admiring the feather while they talk over their day, or sticking toothpicks in the acorns to make tops. A picture of peace. Unlike Yoki's place.

Opposites they may be, but Yoki and Seiichi are best friends. Their friendship might be one of the seven wonders of Kamusari. Countless times I've seen them help each other out at work, not saying much, their minds in perfect sync. When Yoki's up in a cypress tree, lopping off branches, all he has to do is cock his head a little for Seiichi to throw him a rope from the ground. Only then, looking on, does it dawn on me: *Oh, right. That branch hangs over one on the next tree, so unless he supports it with a rope while he cuts it, the weight might cause the other branch to break.*

Sometimes at lunchtime Yoki leans over and helps himself to some of Seiichi's bento. Seiichi usually doesn't say a word, just goes right on eating while Yoki pops the stolen tidbit in his mouth. But when deep-fried chicken—Seiichi's favorite—is involved, then it's another story. Seiichi puts up the lid to his bento box, casually fending off an attack, but Yoki persists, biding his time and stealing a piece with a lightning move (nobody moves faster than Yoki). Then he dashes off, onigiri in hand, the chicken stuffed in his mouth. Seiichi picks up a handful of leaves off the ground and hurls it after him in frustration. Old Man Saburo lets them both have it: "Stop that now! Quit acting childish. You'll get dirt in our food!"

Maybe it's because they're such old friends. Sometimes I get the feeling they're like a couple of kids at play, the same as they must have been years ago. Other times I'll see them talking seriously about work, a pair of adults with perfect mutual understanding. Not having a close friend I've known since childhood, I can't really relate to the nuances of how they communicate.

Imagine spending your childhood with someone from the neighborhood, growing up together and even working together as adults. I doubt if that happens much, if at all, in the city. People go to different schools, different cities even, and grow apart. There are so many different jobs that the chances of working in the same place are slim to none. So watching Yoki and Seiichi together makes me kind of jealous, but at the same time I wonder if all that togetherness isn't a bit suffocating. I start to think maybe I've never had a real friend. I feel disappointed in myself.

Yoki and Seiichi probably think of each other as family. Probably don't sit around pondering the meaning of friendship.

Anyway, on that day on West Mountain, while those two had at it—"You're heartless!" "Why *shouldn't* I first put out the fire?"—I ignored them and ate my onigiri, gazing at a single tree in the distance whose leaves had turned red. It was like the light of a cigarette glowing in the blackness of night, or a ghost fire of legend hovering over a dark sea. There was nothing scary about it, though. It had a beauty that felt comfortable and familiar, a beauty that drew me in.

Right about now, the work isn't as hard as it is in summer, and here I am admiring the fall colors and meditating on the nature of friendship, which is out of character for me. You may think I'm leading a leisurely life, but don't be fooled, people! In fact, lately I've been chasing my tail, driving all around the village in Yoki's pickup. With a shiny, brand-new driver's license tucked in the breast pocket of my work clothes. THE WHOLE VILLAGE WEEPS FOR JOY AT HIS DRIVING SKILLS!—read it like an ad for a movie—EVEN MISCHIEVOUS MONKEYS BOW DOWN AND YIELD THE RIGHT OF WAY!

I'm not one hundred percent sure of myself behind the wheel yet, actually, but I've been driving Yoki's pickup for a while now and have yet to run over any animals (there are more of them than there are humans, and the chances of hitting one are pretty high if you don't watch out). All so that I can transport rice straw.

After the rice is harvested, rice straw is left in the paddies. In the old days they would pile it up, leave it to dry, and then, in the winter, they would sleep on it and use it to weave sandals, light fires, and feed livestock. But nowadays there's little use for it, so mostly it ends up getting incinerated. Demand hasn't dried up entirely, though, and that's where I come in.

I started a delivery service, working evenings after work. I'm trying to save enough money so I can buy my own truck. I load bales of straw in the bed of the pickup and take them wherever they're needed. The village is full of old folks who have a hard time handling straw bales. I get more business than I ever thought I would, thanks to my coworkers, who kindly spread the word: "Just ask, and Yuki will deliver straw to you." Word-of-mouth recommendations are the best.

I make deliveries from paddies on one side of the village to cow-sheds on the other (two local families raise cows); to an old woman whose hobby is weaving straw sandals; to farming families that want to spread straw thickly in their fields to guard against the cold. I make only one or two deliveries a day, but I wouldn't trade this work for anything. Sometimes I stop by Nao's place, and if she feels like it, she'll come with me.

We drive along the village roads as dusk turns to dark. We work together to unload rice straw from the truck, haul it to the client's shed, and pile it up. On the way back, now and then I'll purposely take the long way around. Sometimes we ride in almost total silence, and other times we tell each other funny stories about work.

Sounds like things are zipping along between us, right? It makes me want to roll down the window and crow in triumph, but naturally I refrain. Even though it's just the two of us, sitting close together in the narrow space of the cab, I strive to act natural, like "I'm totally cool with this," and keep the conversation relaxed.

Sometimes Nao comes with me to the parking lot of the Kamusari roadside station and helps me practice my parallel parking, which I'm still pretty lousy at. The roadside station has been taken over by local women, who go there for relaxation. Hardly any other cars are parked there, so I use my imagination. If you want to improve your driving skills in Kamusari, a good imagination is essential: Okay, let's say there's a humongous Benz parked there, the kind that says all over it, *Scratch me and you'll be sorry, mister.*

Nao gets out of the car and gives me instructions: "Back up a foot. Okay, stop. Turn the steering wheel to the right, all the way. Back up five more inches. More, more, okay, okay, stop! Now inch back juuust a little more, while turning the wheel thirty degrees to the left." I have to say, her instructions can be really hard to follow. Sometimes I wonder whether the kids in her class can follow her lessons. But I'm grateful all the same, and I try my best to do as she says. What I have to admire about her is that even when I back up too far and go way over the line, she never gets upset, never raises her voice. She just keeps right on: "Oopsy. All right, let's try that again. Go forward sixty feet and then start backing up."

It's possible she fears for her life, though: she always stands at quite a remove from the pickup while I practice. And when Yoki saw the damage to the rear end of his truck where I bumped into some trees, he laid a hand menacingly on his ax handle and yelled, "What the hell is this, Yuki?" I bravely hid behind Granny Shige, using her as a shield, and repeated "I'm sorry!" a good thirty times.

It's not only this short-term, part-time job that keeps me busy. The whole village is on edge because it's getting to be time for the festival of Oyamazumi-san. Last year they held a grand festival, the kind that comes once every forty-eight years, and I had a hair-raising time. It was the closest I've ever come to death. This year's festival will be a regular one, they tell me, so I can breathe a little easier.

Still, that's regular Kamusari style . . . so we'll still have to get up in the middle of the night, purify ourselves in the river, climb Mt. Kamusari, and cut down a huge tree. A two-hundred-year-old chestnut, I heard. This year, Naka district is in charge. My team, the Seiichi Nakamura team of Kamusari district, will be "leaders." That means that on the night of the festival, we'll go at the head of the procession, carrying staffs and lanterns, guiding the others on that climb up sacred Mt. Kamusari through the pitch-dark forest—just thinking about it fills me with nervous excitement.

The festival has lots of preliminaries. For over a month ahead of time, the villagers carry out various mysterious ceremonies. They put up a scaffold in a rice paddy and dance around it. They string up sacred straw ropes called *shimenawa* over the river, and much more. As the master of Kamusari, Seiichi has to be present at all the ceremonies, so he's a hundred times busier than me.

One evening I was on the road with Nao beside me. We were headed uphill, with the Kamusari River on our left. We'd finished delivering straw for the day; the truck was light, the bed empty of its load. The road curved gently, following the river, and I steered with care. I had good reason to be careful: after swearing over and over to Yoki that I wouldn't cause any more damage, he had finally agreed to let me go on borrowing his pickup.

As we got closer to Nao's house, I saw Seiichi standing in a rice paddy on the right, just ahead. He had parked his own truck by the paddy and was standing alone amid the rice stubble, head down. In the late afternoon sun, his shadow stretched out far across the ground. Something about his silhouette jogged my memory.

"Reminds me of someone . . ." I murmured.

"Kenji Miyazawa," said Nao. "Right?"

Two different reactions crossed my mind: *Dammit, she's still focused on Seiichi* and *That's it! He reminds me of the photo in my high school lit textbook, the one with the caption, "Poet Kenji Miyazawa, walking in a rice paddy."*

I slowed down as we approached. Knowing how Nao feels about Seiichi, I felt I had no choice. I would have preferred to go straight past without stopping, but I didn't want her to think I was small-minded.

"Shall we stop and say hi?" I asked.

To my surprise, she shook her head. "No, let's leave him alone."

Yay! Nao chose me over Seiichi! I wasn't fool enough to think that. Instead I wondered, *What's come over her? This isn't like her at all.* Seiichi's air of loneliness also bothered me.

After we went by, I watched in my rearview mirror as Seiichi's figure grew smaller. He kept standing still, head down, until he vanished behind a curve in the road. What was he doing in a place like that with nightfall setting in? Maybe I should have called out to him after all.

Nao seemed to sense what I was thinking. "He's paying his respects to the god of the rice paddy ahead of the festival for Oyamazumi-san. You mustn't disturb him."

Oh boy, here we go! Another episode in Kamusari folklore. The man I'd worked with in the forest that day and eaten lunch with at noon was standing in a rice paddy in the evening, communing with a god. This side of the Kamusari way of life was too quaint, too fantastical for me—frankly, I couldn't fathom it. But it did arouse my curiosity.

"There's a god for rice paddies?"

"Yeah." Nao nodded. "But he's not always there. Did you see the little *gohei* at Seiichi's feet?"

"Gohei?"

"You know, that little stick with white paper in the shape of lightning. It was stuck in the ground there."

"Didn't notice."

Nao looked at me as if I were none too bright and unfastened her seat belt. We had just arrived at her house. *Today's drive with Nao is over*—the thought made me sad.

But she said, "Want to come in for a cup of tea?"

Yessss! Nao really has *chosen me over Seiichi!* I wasn't fool enough to let her words go to my head that way. Actually, I was afraid she was going to lecture me about something. Or maybe undeserved good luck was a harbinger of pending disaster. I was nervous.

Going inside her house for the first time, I saw it was old but clean and tidy. The small earthen-floor kitchen had a cute little red refrigerator. The six-mat living room had a small, round, low table like the one in Yoki's house. Tacked to a wooden door were drawing upon drawing of Kamusari scenery, evidently her pupils' artwork. They weren't masterpieces, but they did capture the atmosphere of the village.

While she boiled water in the kitchen, I sat at the low table, my heart pounding like I'd just run the hundred-meter dash.

Carrying a steaming teakettle, Nao slipped off her shoes and stepped up into the living room. She filled a pair of teacups and bounced a tea bag up and down in the hot water.

What? Not green tea made in a ceramic teapot, but a tea bag? And one tea bag for both cups of tea? Not that I minded. I love it that she does things the way a guy would. I thanked her for the tea and took an appreciative sip, determined to make it last. The moment I finished the tea, I was sure she'd say, "Okay, you'd better leave now." But she turned on the TV, lit the kerosene stove, turned it in my direction, and generally did all she possibly could to be hospitable.

Yessss!

Could she be lonely, living in that big house all by herself? Old Japanese houses are full of shadows in hallways and corners. As tatami gets old, it can seem oddly springy and soft, and the ceilings issue creaks and rattles. Sometimes at night I'm a little bit scared to go to the toilet in Yoki's house. As I sat across from Nao, sensing the heavy weight of silence in the rooms at my back, such thoughts filled my head. But her mind had gone in a different direction entirely.

"Back to what I was saying before," she said.

I racked my brain—what had she been saying? Something about the god of the rice paddy. *Rather than how to greet a god, let's talk about how to deepen our relationship.* I wanted to make that suggestion, but all I said was "Right."

"The god descends onto the gohei in the paddy. I think Seiichi was addressing the god before. Probably saying something like, *We will be holding the festival for Oyamazumi-san again this year. Please watch over us.* Reporting to the god and asking for his protection."

"Um." I scratched my cheek, unsure how to proceed. "Is Seiichi that kind of person?"

"What do you mean?"

"You know, spiritual, or whatever."

"No, no!" She laughed. "Just the opposite. He's utterly practical. Doesn't believe in the afterworld or horoscopes, either."

"It's always been mysterious to me." I decided to come right out with it. "What do you suppose goes through his mind when he participates in all the village ceremonies? So many Kamusari traditions just seem superstitious to me, or fantastical. I really can't understand them. You're like me, Nao—neither one of us was born here. So, for instance, what do you make of the shimenawa over the river?"

"Well, let me see." She wrapped her hands around her teacup. "To me it's just *there*, like the mountains and the trees and the people."

"So you're a natural girl."

"Are you making fun of me?" She looked annoyed. "It's more than natural, it's like . . ." She thought a moment. "When you see someone you know, you greet them, right? Even if you're in a bad mood for some reason, and even if you don't actually like them very much, you still do, right?"

"Right."

"Greeting people helps to smooth relationships, and it kind of lifts you up, too, I think. Kamusari ceremonies are an extension of that. Just like in the morning you tell people *'Good morning,'* people here offer specific greetings at specific times of year to the gods, whose presence they take for granted. That's how I see it."

I still didn't quite get it.

"And besides," she went on, "Seiichi is the master, after all."

"Meaning that as the village leader, he has to uphold tradition?"

"Yes. He has a really strong sense of responsibility, you know."

She loved that about him—I could tell from the look on her face. A sense of responsibility, huh? How could someone like me, just drifting through life, develop a strong sense of responsibility?

"He became master when he was still in high school. Think of it." She said the words slowly. "He had no choice but to take that on. It must all be so different for him than it is for you or me."

"Huh?" How could anyone in high school become master of the village? It meant taking full charge of Nakamura Lumber, supervising the management of a vast amount of forestland, earning the villagers' respect. Seiichi must have been a super-achiever in high school. "Is it because his father died young?"

"You don't know anything, do you?" She looked surprised. "It's not just his parents. Remember, Yoki has no parents, either."

"Wait. Are you telling me that Seiichi and Yoki are both love children of the god of Kamusari?"

"That's absurd and you know it."

She was right. Being in this secluded mountain village, so full of traditions and festivals I'd never seen or heard of back in Yokohama, I got carried away for a moment. So Seiichi's parents had both died young. It *had* occurred to me that not many people in the village were in their fifties, the age Yoki's parents would have been.

"I've said too much." She finished her tea. "It's starting to get dark out. You'd better head back."

Tell me about Seiichi's and Yoki's parents. I asked her with my eyes, but she pretended not to notice. I thanked her for the tea and reluctantly got to my feet.

Nao went down into the entryway and saw me off. I stepped outside, and the door shut unceremoniously behind me. But just before it closed, I heard her whisper:

"If you want to know more, go to the graveyard."

The next day was Saturday, a day off. Santa came over in the morning. We pretended to swim in my room. All we did was crawl around on our bellies, waving our arms and legs, and dive off a pile of folded futons and quilts in the corner, but depending on the grain of the tatami, we could really slide. Santa loved it and got pretty excited, rolling around and laughing himself silly.

After we'd used up some of our energy that way, it was time for ten o'clock tea. Granny Shige brought out sesame rice crackers for us. She ate hers by dunking them in her tea and sucking on them.

Miho went out back to call Yoki. He was swinging his ax like a demon, chopping firewood, apparently. It looked like winter would come early, so he must have decided to start laying in a good supply. He had used way more energy than Santa and me, but when he came in, he was his usual energetic self. He took off his sweat-soaked shirt, and his muscular body gave off steam. As soon as he threw on a clean shirt, he bit into three hard rice crackers piled on top of each other. I had a hard time biting through one.

"What's your daddy up to?" Yoki asked Santa, remembering his manners.

"This morning he was watching TV with Mommy and going over the books."

"That's nice. Your folks get along great, huh."

This seemed like a doubtful assumption to me. Watching TV together has nothing to do with getting along or not; it's a pretty typical way for any couple to spend a day off. But then, Yoki was in constant danger of opening hostilities with Miho, so maybe his standard for marital bliss was low.

"Daddy said he's going shopping in Tsu this afternoon. I want to go, too, so I can go to the bookstore. I'll go home now."

After this announcement, Santa added politely, "Thanks for the tea, Granny Shige. And Yu-chan, I'll come again." He spoke to me gravely, as if to say, *I have to go, but don't be sad.*

I almost burst out laughing, but I made an effort to look disappointed. "Yeah, come over and we'll play again."

Granny Shige had dozed off where she sat, nodding. Yoki, perhaps deciding to follow Seiichi's example, turned on the TV. Not five minutes later, he and Miho were bickering over the female announcer on the screen.

"Eri's cute! You can't see straight," he said.

"No, you can't *think* straight. What's cute about a woman who goes, 'Gee, I dunno'? Sounds as if she had a brain meltdown. She's as artificial as they come. And anyway, what kind of an announcer is asked to comment and goes, 'Gee, I dunno'?"

"Oh, she was just being honest. It's cute. I like her face, too, the way she looks like a stunned raccoon dog."

"Oh, really. Excuse *me* for not having a face like a raccoon dog!"

"Don't be silly. Your face may not be the same type as Eri's, but it's smack in the strike zone of what I like."

"What a thing to say!" Blushing, Miho reached out and caught Granny Shige just as she was about to bonk her forehead on the table.

Being around those two wore me out. I decided to leave them to their happy bickering. "I'm going for a walk."

My destination was the graveyard, a fifteen-minute walk from Yoki's place. On one side of the road there was a densely forested mountain, and on the other was the river. As I walked along, I noticed that the trees would soon need thinning and that the current was pretty swift. A silver fish leaping in the air took me by surprise. At first the air felt cold and I hunched my shoulders, but after a while I got used to it.

Soon I spotted the little graveyard up ahead. It was nestled by the river, where there was plenty of sun but the wind blew cold. Mt. Kamusari was directly across from it. The spirits of people who were born and died in Kamusari eventually travel beyond Mt. Kamusari, I'd heard.

I walked among the gravestones while the wind wreaked havoc on my hair. The markers were all the same size and height. The village was small; they were probably careful to keep them all the same. The white gravel underfoot was well raked, and nearly every grave was adorned with a fresh green branch of star anise.

Seiichi's family grave was way in the back. It appeared to contain a number of old graves from the days before cremation, brought here from somewhere else. Next to shiny, vertical granite gravestones were a number of smaller mossy graves. Those were Seiichi's ancestors, descended, according to lore, from the offspring of Nagahiko, the snake god, and his human bride.

I held my palms together in respect before the granite monuments and looked at the posthumous Buddhist names of Seiichi's parents, chiseled down the side. I'd never met them, so I didn't feel anything in particular.

Next, I looked around for Yoki's family grave. Again, posthumous Buddhist names were engraved along with their actual names. Yoki's parents I felt I knew a little bit from seeing their faces on the family altar all the time, so I did feel a twinge of sadness. Still, I didn't really know what to think. The wind was chilling me through. I shivered.

Something tugged at my awareness. What was it? I looked once more at the engravings on the stones. It wasn't the names that bothered me, but the dates of death. His father and mother had died on the exact same day. What were the chances of a husband and wife getting sick and dying on the same day? Pretty low. Maybe there'd been an accident or something.

I quickly went back to Seiichi's family grave. His parents had died on the same day as Yoki's.

What could it mean?

I took a deep breath, steadied myself, and went around the grave-yard, checking all the gravestones. In all, sixteen people had died on May 6, twenty years before.

Kamusari, the peaceful village where living was easy. Kamusari, ringed by mountains of lush green and blessed by a river of clear, pure water. In this village filled with unceasing signs of life—the playful chirping of birds in the treetops, the sound of animals darting through the brush, the gleam of fish in the water, reflecting sunlight—what had gone wrong?

For sixteen people in one village all to die on the exact same day was not normal.

I thought back to Seiichi's brooding figure in the paddy at twilight. He'd seemed weighed down by a crushing load of loneliness and sadness. Yet he'd stood firmly on the ground, quietly looking down, as if seeing invisible things and hearing soundless sounds.

I need to know, I thought. If I were to go on living in Kamusari, it wasn't enough to learn only the appealing bits of village lore, the fantastical stories. The sadness and pain the villagers had experienced was also something I wanted to know about.

But how and when could I broach such a topic? I realized all over again that I'd never had a friend I could really open up to. I'd only thought about having a good time. The desire to share something with someone in order to walk alongside them forever was new to me. And so now, at this crucial moment, I had no idea how to approach people who were important to me, how to be truthful and open with them.

Still, I've got to do it. Readers, give me courage! And yes, I know—I have no readers, and despite the meaning of my name, I have no courage, either. I know, I know. Ah, what should I do?

It was midafternoon, but I stood for a while in the windy graveyard without stirring, as if I'd lost my way in the dark of night.

4

THE FOURTH NIGHT

MISHAP AND DISASTER IN KAMUSARI

"At night in the mountains," Yoki said, "I feel a presence."

"A presence? Like what?" I asked in a low voice. I hoped he wasn't about to tell a scary story.

Yoki threw a small branch on the fire. The flames flared up momentarily, casting a reddish light on his face as he sat with his eyes downturned. High in the cedars, the wind sighed. Noko, curled up next to Yoki, looked up anxiously, and Yoki patted him on the head. "I can't really explain it, but it's like somebody's watching me. Calling my name, like they know me."

I felt a twinge of fear and wrapped myself tighter in the blanket.

Yoki laughed. "It's nothing scary. It's a familiar presence. Could be villagers who've passed, or the god of the mountain. Or both, like they've joined together. A spirit or spirits of some kind. Don't you feel it, too, right now?"

I closed my eyes and listened. The wind had stopped and the mountain was silent, as if wrapped in a giant muffler. I focused all my attention, and thought I heard murmurs beyond the silence. What was being said, I couldn't tell. It was as if countless people (?) had gathered together and were all speaking, each in their own way. But the collective murmur wasn't loud. It was like whispers or moaning.

Quickly I opened my eyes. If I didn't, I was afraid I might be drawn into the darkest, deepest part of night and disappear.

Across the campfire I could see Yoki's face. He was sitting cross-legged on the ground, his figure half dissolving into the darkness behind, poking the fire with the handle of his ax as he waited for morning.

Yoki and I were more or less stranded on South Mountain.

Stranded? Yuki, are you okay? Some of my readers, especially you ladies, may be alarmed. Dry those tears. I'm sitting here writing this, which proves I got home safely from the mountain. Also, yes, I am well aware that I'm writing this all alone on Yoki's computer, and there aren't any ladies, er, readers. I haven't lost my mind, so you can relax on that score.

Actually, I wanted to write with detail and ambiance about how we got stranded on the mountain, so you'd feel as if you were there. (The word *ambiance* is one I'm not used to using, by the way, and it didn't just pop into my head, either. It took a good five minutes of cogitating before I hit on it.) Sort of like on-the-scene reporting: *Will Yuki make it down the mountain? Stay tuned for more!* That's more exciting for the (nonexistent) readers, right?

But it's no use. Because I *did* make it down the mountain, and I'm writing this well after the fact, and you all know it. Anyway, I'll go ahead and tell what happened. How Yoki and I got into trouble and how we came out of it alive. You already know the ending, so this won't be as thrilling as it might have been, but here goes.

The other day, in mid-November, we had the Oyamazumi festival. (For more information about the festival, check the computer file marked "The Easy Life in Kamusari.") It started in the middle of the night with a purifying dip in the Kamusari River. The water was so cold it hurt. It felt as if a congregation of gigantic alligators was closing in on me, biting me all over. I lost the power of speech. All I could do was make a weird sound like a combination of whistling and laughing. My lungs, bronchial tubes, and diaphragm cramped, and despite myself, that peculiar sound was all I could produce.

Old Man Saburo is in his late seventies, and I worried that his heart might not withstand the shock, but he was in his element. He soaked in the current up to his neck, fully dressed, with his eyes closed. From the look on his face, I half expected him to sigh, "Ah, this feels good!" as if he were in a hot spring. For all I could tell, he was halfway to the next world—soaking in the Sanzu River, the one the souls of the dead must cross. I begged him silently: *Old Man Saburo, don't stay in too long! Get out of the river!* Yoki, meanwhile, was chanting loudly and splashing bucketfuls of icy water over his head with so much vigor, he might as well have been meditating under a waterfall. As usual, he had way more stamina and drive than a normal person. I just left him to himself.

After the purification ritual, we gathered on the bank and changed into white garb like what *yamabushi* wear. (Yamabushi are ascetic mountain hermits who supposedly have supernatural powers.) While we walked from the river to the foot of Mt. Kamusari, talking wasn't allowed. All the Kamusari woodsmen—there are about forty of us—walked silently in lines. Since the Nakamura team members were the leaders this year, we headed the procession, carrying lanterns and metal staffs with interlocking rings on the end that jangled with every step.

The darkness on the road was profound. Apart from the lantern light casting a reddish glow on our hands and feet, we couldn't see anything at all. The darkness formed a kind of wall, blocking the way ahead. It was like trying to cut steel by holding a match to it. After a while I couldn't have said whether we were moving ahead or walking in place or going backward. The metallic jangle of the staffs melted into the depths of the night like widening ripples on a lake. There were no turns on the way to Mt. Kamusari, so we couldn't lose our way, and yet

I became anxious and peered at the faces of Seiichi and Yoki, walking beside me. Their intent expressions emerged faintly out of the darkness.

The ground felt cold through my *jikatabi,* the rubber-soled, split-toed shoes I always wear on the mountains. The rustle of leaves spread from mountain to mountain like murmurs. The stars overhead shone like silver music.

When we reached the foot of Mt. Kamusari, we each picked up equipment left there for us by the man from the forestry cooperative (Wild Boar Stew Guy, I used to call him, because he made stew for me on my first night in Kamusari; now I call him Wild Boar Guy). I put on a helmet, slung a pair of goggles around my neck, and fastened my trusty chain saw across my back. Yoki tucked his ax in his obi. Noko joined us at the foot of the mountain. He must have come running from home.

The staffs served as walking sticks, but because we each held a lantern, too, our hands were full, which made climbing all the harder. As leaders, we couldn't rest along the way. We had to keep up a steady pace, neither too fast nor too slow, and make our way up the overgrown trail. Since Mt. Kamusari is the sacred dwelling of Oyamazumi-san, as a rule no one sets foot on it except during the festival. The path isn't kept up. There was nothing for it but to trudge straight up the mountainside through the grasses and shrubs, pushing branches aside. Unlike roads that wind up a mountain, the route we took was incredibly steep, and gradually we ran out of breath. Noko's tongue was hanging out.

Mt. Kamusari at night was filled with the sound of our breathing, the jangle of the staffs, the flicker of lantern light. Yoki, as usual, had the most energy, charging up the mountainside in the lead. At the sound of his coming, startled rabbits and weasels in the bushes darted off, and birds in the trees made a sleepy-sounding racket.

"Has he no fear?" I murmured.

As no tree planting takes place on Mt. Kamusari, all varieties of trees grow together to form a dense forest. There were plenty of the giant trees classed as shimboku, divine trees; walking among them even in the daytime would be daunting. Plus, the forest is home to lots of birds and animals; we could sense their presence in the darkness and see their eyes shining. Since they hide behind trees and in the brush, even in daylight you seldom see them—but they were definitely there. All kinds of nonhuman living creatures.

"What's that?" Iwao, behind me, had overheard my muttered comment.

"Yoki." Taking care not to put out my lantern, I shifted my weight and moved the chain saw on my back to a more comfortable position. "The way he runs ahead, all by himself. What if he comes on a bear? Does he ever think about that?"

"Probably not." Iwao chuckled. "Even if he ran into a brown bear, he'd probably just pick it up and toss it aside."

He was right. I could imagine Yoki outwrestling a bear. Okay, a brown bear might be too much for him, but a medium-sized black bear? He could throw it over his shoulder and then get it in a spinal lock, standing over it and hooking its legs in his arms.

"Besides," Iwao said, "we purified ourselves for Oyamazumi-san, and now we're headed up the mountain to pay our respects. I'll bet you Mr. Bear knows it and is lying low on purpose, just keeping quiet in his house."

There it was again, the fairy-tale side of Kamusari. Gods and humans and animals, all the same. It gave me a strange feeling to hear Iwao, a tough middle-aged guy, talk about the bear's "house"—let alone use the expression "Mr. Bear"! I remembered that Iwao had been spirited away as a small child. That had made him strong. He'd been chosen by the god of Kamusari. If he thought Mr. Bear was lying low, then there was nothing to worry about.

We arrived at the foot of the chestnut tree before dawn. My mouth fell open.

When I hear *chestnut tree*, I think of a nice little tree standing in a grove, six and a half to ten feet tall, tops. Right? The nuts are delicious, but the flowers smell disgusting. That's about it. The Kamusari chestnut was totally different in scale. It was huge—easily sixty-five feet tall. Its girth was huge, too. Two men with their arms spread out couldn't have reached all the way around. And the bark was amazing: it had a dark sheen, as if it had been smoked, and dozens of deep vertical furrows. It was imposing. It was erotic. It was both at once, and it towered over that hillside with such commanding presence that it made you want to fall on your knees.

Not only did the tree have no flowers or nuts, it had shed most of its leaves, and I was glad of it. If, on top of everything else, it had been giving off that disgusting smell, I would have been so overcome I'd have started laughing. Not because it was funny. I mean the kind of helpless laughter that bubbles up in the face of unimaginable terror or awe.

Our team had been charged with the responsibility of leading everyone to the chestnut tree. Now that we had done that, we could sit back and watch the rest of the proceedings. The teams responsible this time for cutting down the tree began to confer. This was some festival, I thought, since it involved cutting down a tree of such magnitude every year.

I sat by an oak tree a little distance away and waited for the conference to end. The other two teams were arguing heatedly about which direction to fell the tree in. As usual, the intensity of the argument was softened, to my ears, anyway, by the Kamusari drawl. Yoki wasn't involved, but he stuck his nose in, declaring irresponsibly, "Why not just fell the chestnut in the direction it wants to go?"

Seiichi and Old Man Saburo were pouring sake around the foot of the tree and intoning some sort of prayer. Iwao was stroking the green moss on the bark of the tree and nodding to himself. Or could he be . . . communing with the spirit of the tree?

The morning sun came up, its beams lighting up the forest. Leaves and branches of every color and shape were touched with pale gold in the pure morning air. The trilling of the birds was every bit as loud as the human voices. I blew out my lantern, folded it, and tucked it in my obi.

I glanced to my side, and there sat Mr. Yamane. I choked. Lately he's warmed to me a little, but I'm still uncomfortable around him. He strikes me as a stubborn guy who lives for work. Also, he's unfriendly. When I first came, if I saw him on the street and said hello, he just ignored me. He has no use for people whose commitment to forestry is half-hearted. I get that. The other day, he saw me out on a pickup-truck date (?) with Nao. After that, he waited till he saw me out walking by myself, called me over, and warned, "Don't you start flirting and carrying on." This from a guy who normally only grunts at me. He's kind of mean. But not a bad person underneath, I think.

There under the oak tree I decided to stand my ground—only, of course, I was sitting. Before Mr. Yamane had a chance to say anything, I stole a look at him. He was patting the breast of his yamabushi top. Casually wondering what he might have in there, I looked down and nearly yelped in surprise. Poking out of the breast was the face of a bizarre-looking creature. It looked dried and blackish. A mummified monkey? A tree root for making Chinese medicine?

"Curious?" he asked.

"Yes. What is that?"

"I'll show you."

With an air of importance, he drew out the queer-looking thing. It was five inches or so long, wrapped in a thin white towel. Only the face was visible, which made it all the eerier. I composed myself and took a closer look. It was some kind of fish, but the face was scary. The skin (scales?) was bumpy, the eyes bugged out, the big mouth hung open, and the cheeks were swollen. Were there actual fish that looked like this? Maybe it wasn't a mummified monkey but a mummified mermaid.

Drawing back, I continued to examine the mysterious object as Mr. Yamane slowly removed the towel. Then I could see the mummy in its entirety. It was definitely a fish. The pectoral fins were shaped like fans and the dorsal fins formed ridges, like on a dinosaur.

"It's a devil stinger."

I repeated the name, wonderingly. It was a kind of fish I'd heard of but never tasted. More important, why bring a dried fish to the mountain? Emergency rations? A favorite snack? Mr. Yamane seemed to realize I was giving off question marks right and left. He quickly explained.

"Oyamazumi-san is said to have two daughters. The younger one is a great beauty, but her sister is . . . you know."

"Ugly?"

"Ssshh!" He clapped a hand over my mouth. "Don't ever use a word like that on the mountain."

"Why not?"

"You're only going to upset the older sister. That's why I bring the devil stinger here, to make her feel better. Because the devil stinger is ug—aesthetically challenged, too. The goddess takes one look and says to herself, *Wow, there's somebody with a face that's ugli—more aesthetically challenged than mine.* She's all smiles. So we can get on with our work in peace."

There it was again, I thought. Kamusari superstition. At the same time, I was intrigued. The goddess sounded so human. And how resourceful of humans to resort to psychological warfare against the gods!

I gave the devil stinger a tentative poke. It felt dry and hard to the touch. Now that I got a good look at it, there was something appealing about its looks. Probably the elder daughter of Oyamazumi-san only thought herself ugly, too. Beauty is in the eye of the beholder, they say; I bet the right person would find her attractive.

I thought back to last year's festival, when I'd seen two mysterious women in kimonos, one red, the other white, floating near the top of the giant cedar. I had convinced myself my eyes were playing tricks on me, but what if those actually *had* been the daughters of Oyamazumi-san? I toyed with the idea. Living in the village had steeped me in the world of fairy tales.

"At last year's festival, I had a hell of a time, you may recall," said Mr. Yamane.

His voice brought me back to reality. This would never do. Kimono-clad women didn't levitate and go drifting off. I'd been hallucinating, I told myself sternly, and redirected my attention to what Mr. Yamane was saying.

"That's right. You got blown off the log." What a horrifying moment that had been! The festival last year had been a life-and-death struggle. I'd never wanted anything to do with it again, and yet here I was, participating for the second time in a row.

"The way I see it, that must be because I did something to anger the god of the mountain. That's why I brought the devil stinger this year. I tucked it in my top and came in a spirit of humility."

Humility? Mr. Yamane? The combination seemed as strange as eel and pickled plum, or watermelon and tempura. Though if he really *had* acquired humility, how great would that be?

He carefully rewrapped the dried devil stinger and tucked it back inside his top. I looked over at the chestnut tree. They had finally decided on the direction. The one chosen to fell it switched on his chain saw.

"*Keh!*" This was the signal that meant "I'm starting to chop it down!"

"*Hoina!*" the men shouted in response. "Okay, go!"

The chain saw touched the bark of the chestnut tree, sending white wood chips and sawdust flying. Everyone stood up. Mr. Yamane and I stood up, too, and watched the felling of the beautiful tree. As the blade of the chain saw bit into the tree, the men launched into a rhythmic chorus. They did it to encourage the one cutting down the tree, and also as a tribute to the tree itself. After all, it had endured through two centuries of rain and wind. It had earned a send-off of highest respect.

Eventually, the tree came crashing to the ground. The trunk didn't crack, and the tree didn't go sliding down the mountain. The operation was a success. Yoki ran toward the fallen tree in high spirits. The branches had to be removed, as they would get in the way when carrying the tree off the mountain. Seiichi and Old Man Saburo were talking over where to cut in order to maximize the value of the lumber. Everyone's attention was focused on the chestnut tree.

A sudden idea came to me: maybe now I could ask Mr. Yamane how Seiichi's and Yoki's parents had died. I didn't feel at all close to him; he and I had never hit it off. But today, he'd shown me the dried devil stinger and told me why he brought it here. That was a sign he was willing to meet me halfway, wasn't it? I didn't feel comfortable broaching the sensitive topic with my teammates or Yoki's family. Not being close to Mr. Yamane somehow made me feel he was the one person I could ask.

I sidled closer to Mr. Yamane and whispered in his ear: "There's something I want to ask you."

"Eh? What is it? That tickles!" He rubbed his ear and looked up at me questioningly.

"The other day I went to the graveyard. What happened in the village on May 6, twenty years ago?"

"What do you want to know a thing like that for?" His expression grew severe.

I wasn't asking out of mere curiosity. Of course I *was* curious, but my need to know came from a much deeper place.

"I owe Seiichi and Yoki so much," I said. How could I convey to Mr. Yamane all that I had been thinking the past few days? I struggled to find words. "But as it is, I don't really know them. I feel like I'll never measure up. And with me knowing nothing about what happened,

Seiichi and Yoki can't share their feelings with me when they're in pain. It kills me to think I can never really be there for them."

Mr. Yamane patted the devil stinger tucked in his breast. For a while he was silent. By now the branches were stripped from the chestnut tree, and it had been transformed into an easily transportable log.

"There's something called a *ko*," he said all of a sudden. "People put in money toward a group project like shrine repair or travel. Ever hear of it?"

"No."

"No, I suppose you wouldn't have. Ever since the accident, the village gave them up." He sighed. "It was something like a cooperative or a club. In Kamusari, *Omine-ko* was popular."

The word *accident* jumped out at me, and what on earth was Omine-ko? I cocked my head, puzzled, and Mr. Yamane explained. I'll sum up what he said.

Northwest of Kamusari, past the border with Nara prefecture, there is a sacred mountain called Mt. Omine that's associated with the Shugendo sect of Buddhism. It's been a center of faith from ancient times, and some Kamusari villagers go there to worship at least once a year. "My old man took me there when I was eighteen," Mr. Yamane recalled. "Had to crawl along a steep cliff without a lifeline. He said to me, *Are you going to start acting like an adult? If not, I'll kick you over the edge of this cliff right now!* I didn't want to go over the edge, so I said, 'I will! I promise!'"

Mt. Omine is off-limits to women, apparently, but they're allowed to go near it for sightseeing. The villagers went there together, combining tourism and spirituality. The purpose of Omine-ko was to raise money for the trip.

"Twenty years ago, the members set off from Kamusari for Nara. They hired a microbus. And then . . ." Mr. Yamane dropped his eyes. "On the way home there was an accident. Somewhere deep in the mountains, the driver must've swerved to avoid hitting a deer. The bus plunged to the bottom of a valley, killing everyone aboard. Sixteen people from the village died, along with the driver. Seiichi's and Yoki's parents were on board. Most of the dead were from our district, people taken in the prime of life. The only ones of our generation who survived were Miho's parents, who stayed home because they had the store to run; Iwao, who canceled his reservation because he had a stomachache; and me. I stayed home to look after my mother."

So that's what had happened. Scarcely able to process what I had heard, I stood speechless. Where had the god of Kamusari been that day? Didn't his protection extend to sightseeing trips across the prefectural border? In view of all those who had met sudden death, and those whose family and friends had been snatched away, the idea of a festival to honor Oyamazumi-san now seemed hollow and pointless.

"A lot happened, but it's been twenty years. Let it rest, and don't stir up anything." Mr. Yamane patted me on the shoulder and walked off toward what remained of the chestnut tree, which was now wrapped in layers of blankets. A large peg had been pounded into either end. What? We hadn't wrapped last year's thousand-year-old log in blankets. What was going on?

The next moment, I heard a deafening roar and felt a mighty blast of wind. I looked up and saw a white copter with a blue line running through it hovering over the treetops. The trees swayed; leaves and dust swirled in the air. I put on my goggles and stuck my fingers in my ears.

Yoki ran under the helicopter, crouched over; the sight reminded me of countless scenes from war movies. The others rushed to join him. They fastened cables hanging from the helicopter to the pegs on either end of the chestnut trunk. Then the helicopter slowly rose and flew toward South Mountain, taking the tree with it.

When all was quiet again, I spoke up. "Gee. So you can carry out the tree by helicopter!"

"Yup." Yoki looked satisfied as he watched the helicopter grow smaller in the sky. "It went quick and smooth this time."

"Then why not use a helicopter in the grand festival, too? Why'd we have to risk our lives last year?"

"Don't be an idiot. The grand festival is special. Using a copter for that would make Oyamazumi-san angry."

His answer disappointed me. Ignoring the slump of my shoulders, Yoki called: "Okay, everybody, let's go drink!"

At the foot of Mt. Kamusari, the women of the village joined us, and the party went on till all hours.

Anyway, one way or another, this year's Oyamazumi festival had come safely to an end. That's what I thought, but of course, I was in for a surprise.

Two days after the festival, the Nakamura team set off for South Mountain. (The day after the festival, so many people were hung over, you could hear groaning all over the village.) The chestnut tree that had been airlifted was lying on the hillside and needed to be recovered. As long as they were going to hire a helicopter, it seemed to me they might as well have arranged for it to fly the tree all the way to its destination, the lumber market. But apparently that would have cost a fortune, and getting it from Mt. Kamusari to the neighboring South Mountain was the best they could do.

On the day of the festival, the team of witnesses waited on South Mountain for the helicopter to arrive. Once the huge piece of wood was safely lowered onto the road and the cables unhooked, they came back and joined the festivities. As long as the tree was lying there on the road, it seemed to me they might as well have loaded it onto a truck and driven it off then and there. But the villagers take a relaxed approach to life, and the lure of sake was enough to bring the work to a standstill.

When we had all recovered from our hangovers, it fell to the Nakamura team to go and retrieve the chestnut tree. The road on South Mountain goes midway up the mountain, so getting where we needed to go was no problem. Wild Boar Guy from the cooperative drove a heavy truck to convey the tree, and we used a crane to hoist it onto the bed of the truck. We finished before noon and off he drove, expertly negotiating the narrow road.

I folded the blankets and piled them in the bed of Yoki's truck. It was lunchtime, so I sat on the pile and ate my jumbo onigiri. Noko was begging to join me, so I lifted him up. His lunch was a drawstring bag of dry dog food. Yoki munched on his onigiri while standing in the road, talking something over with Seiichi. He nodded several times and then came over to the pickup.

"This afternoon you and I are setting off on foot."

"Okay. Where to?"

"Next mountain over, there are some high-voltage towers. A maintenance team is coming to inspect 'em, so we need to check on the condition of the path. Nobody's been on it for years. No telling what shape it's in."

"How long will it take?"

"Two hours each way."

I looked up. There were no clouds, but the sky had a wintry cast, and sunset wasn't far off. We needed to get going.

"All right, let's go."

I stuffed the rest of the onigiri in my mouth and jumped to the ground, holding Noko.

Only Yoki and I were going to the towers—and Noko, too. Seiichi, Iwao, and Old Man Saburo would stay behind and work on South Mountain. Before we could plant cedar and cypress saplings there, the clear-cut slope had to be readied.

I figured they picked me to go with Yoki because I was young and had good, strong legs. It was a nice feeling. When I first joined the team, I couldn't keep pace with the others; I'd no doubt been a terrible burden. And now with a four-hour hike to be made, they turned to me. I climbed the mountainside, full of motivation.

Unlike Mt. Kamusari, here the path showed faint signs of human use, and it was winding rather than straight up. I couldn't quite hum like Yoki as I went, but I managed just fine, thank you. Every so often Noko would veer off into the bushes, following a scent. Yoki kept an eye on the terrain, kicking aside stones that might get in someone's way. When he led the inspectors to the towers, the last thing he wanted was for someone to get lost or injured.

Along the way, we passed under the zelkova I'd heard about, the sacred one. We removed our helmets and bowed our heads. The zelkova stood with silent dignity, spreading its branches wide. It was magnificent.

About ninety minutes after we started out, just as we were crossing the valley between the two mountains, Yoki said, "Could be a bear around here."

"You're kidding, right?"

"Nope." He pointed toward the stream. "That's a thirty-year-old cedar over there, and the bark's been stripped. A bear did that."

"Not a deer?"

"Wasn't stripped too long ago. It goes up too high for a deer. It's a bear, all right."

"Now what do we do?" Scared, I stuck close behind Yoki.

He shook his head as if to say, *Could be bad.* "If a bear comes near us, Noko'll start to howl. All we can do is fight it off with the chain saw and ax."

"I'd rather run for it."

Yoki gave a dry smile. "When you run away from a bear, don't turn your back on it. Go as fast as you can, running backward."

"That sounds awfully hard."

"Like this. Watch."

Without turning around, Yoki reversed course—not moving from the waist up. He moved so fast, it was weird. I don't know how to describe it. Okay, think of a Noh actor. You know the way they slide their feet forward? Like that, only eight times faster and backward. It didn't look human. I burst out laughing.

Yoki shifted gears nonchalantly, came back, and started walking ahead of me again. "Bears go into hibernation right about this time of year, so we should be all right."

I wondered for a moment if he'd put on that demonstration just to ease my nerves, but I quickly dismissed the idea. Yoki wasn't one to cater to people's nerves. He did as he pleased at all times, following his instincts. Probably he'd just felt like running backward for no reason. Yoki could cause trouble, and he was a source of constant worry, but at the same time he was never boring. He might be a reckless son of a gun, but I knew of no one who didn't like him.

We reached the towers in less than two hours. The area hadn't been planted with trees, and it was overrun with ferns. The view was breathtaking: layer upon layer of rippling green mountains. I wish you all could have seen it. The few clouds in the sky cast shadows so dark green, they were nearly black, moving in slow patches across the rugged terrain.

For a while, Yoki and I hacked away at ferns. The towers stood in a line across the ridge, roughly a thousand feet apart.

"We'll have to come back with more people to clean out these ferns," said Yoki.

It was going to take a pretty long time just to clear the area around one tower. We had checked the path, and the sun was sinking, so we decided to call it a day.

After spending less than an hour by the towers, we started back. Noko came along, tearing in and out of thickets along the way. We passed safely by the stream where a bear had come and gone.

By the time we made it back to the peak of South Mountain, it was past four o'clock. Cedars blocked the sun, so it was already starting to get dark.

I was in a hurry to get back to the road before the sun set. Also, my guard was down. We were more than halfway back, we hadn't run into any bears, and I'd been able to keep up with Yoki. I must have relaxed my focus.

It happened just when we came to the sacred zelkova. A loud rustling in the bushes off to one side startled me and put me on the defensive. My right foot caught in a hollow in the ground, causing me to twist my ankle hard. I cried out in pain and fell over, just as Noko was emerging from the bushes. He looked at me in surprise, came over, and sniffed my cheek.

Yoki immediately turned back. "What happened?" he asked, crouching beside me and checking me all over with calm eyes and hands.

"It's my ankle." I sat up, but the ankle hurt so much I couldn't get to my feet. Still sitting on the slope, I pulled off my spiked jikatabi and rolled up the leg of my pants. Already, the ankle was badly swollen.

"You sure it's not broken? Try to move it." I did, and he decided it was probably a sprain.

"What'll we do? I'm sorry, Yoki."

Without a word, he gave me a pat on the head and stood up. For a few moments he stood looking up at the sky through the leaves, and then he looked back down at me. "I wish I could carry you, but it'd be dark before we got back. Too risky. We'll spend the night here."

I flinched. "But the bear . . ."

"It won't come out." I wondered how he could be so sure, but he sounded positive. "Animals know when they're licked. No bear's dumb enough to come out just to get its ass kicked by me."

I wasn't convinced, but Yoki swung into action. He took his phone out of his breast pocket. "I don't know if it'll connect," he muttered. "I hope it does. Come on, come on . . ."

Then I heard Seiichi's voice: "Yoki? What happened?"

"Yuki twisted his ankle. Nah, just a sprain, I think. Yup, that's right, halfway down South Mountain. Right by the zelkova. The sun's going down, so we'll stay here and wait for morning. Do me a favor, would you? Bring us the blankets and cigarette lighter in my truck. Thanks."

He turned to me. "I'm going to walk back to that stream and get us some water. You and Noko stay here."

"But it's almost dark. It's not safe."

"It'll be fine. Take the blankets when Seiichi gets here."

Yoki grabbed my helmet and set off. There wasn't time for him to carry me down the mountain before nightfall. But he clearly thought that Seiichi and he could move quickly on their own, unencumbered by me, one traveling from the zelkova to the stream and back, the other from the road to the zelkova and back.

Unable to walk, I sat on the slope with Noko and waited. My right ankle felt hot and beat with a strong pulse, as if my heart had moved there; the pulsations hurt. There was less than an hour before dark, I judged. It had taken me just under an hour to climb from the zelkova to the stream; now Yoki was going to make the round trip in the same amount of time. I had congratulated myself on keeping pace with him, but he'd been matching his pace to mine the whole time. I was ashamed of my arrogant assumption and mad at myself for getting injured.

Soon a flashlight shone, and Seiichi's voice sounded: "Hey there, Yuki! You okay?" He had made the climb in twenty minutes. It had taken me half an hour. This didn't cheer me any. I might be younger than Seiichi and Yoki, but my legs were no match for theirs.

"I'm fine. Sorry."

Seiichi's figure emerged from the dusk. When he dropped the blankets he'd been carrying, out spilled a large number of branches. Figuring we would need firewood, he had gathered them along the way. How like him.

Using the branches, Seiichi lit a fire, and then examined my ankle in the firelight.

"It's pretty swollen."

"Yoki went to get some water."

"Have you got a face towel? I'll leave one here, so use it to keep the ankle cold. You might get feverish, so stay warm, and stay put." He wrapped me in a blanket and had me lean against the zelkova. The trunk blocked the wind, and with the fire right in front of me, I didn't feel cold.

Seiichi turned to the tree and placed his palms together in reverence. "Watch over Yuki and Yoki," he said softly.

What am I supposed to do when I have to take a leak? I wondered suddenly. I couldn't possibly relieve myself here by the sacred tree; I'd have to hop over to a nearby cedar.

"Oh, Seiichi, you're here." Yoki was carrying the helmet carefully in both hands. "Thanks a lot."

"I brought the lighter and some cookies I found lying around." Seiichi handed them over to Yoki. "Shall I stay?"

"No, that's okay. You're the only one who knows where we are. Go home and wait to hear from us in the morning. If we're not back by eight, call for help."

"All right. Watch out, now. Take care of Yuki."

"Will do."

Flashlight in hand, Seiichi started back down the dark slope, turning to look back every so often. His back soon disappeared from view. I was amazed at his speed. Maybe the men of Kamusari really were tengu, the mythical birdmen said to inhabit Japan's mountains and forests.

Yoki set the helmet on the ground and secured it in place with stones. He soaked a thin towel in the water, then took out an oval leaf from his pants pocket. "It's a loquat leaf. Granny Shige always says an infusion made from this is good for a sprain. I can't boil water now, so I'll just wrap it over the ankle."

I sincerely doubted that this would have any effect, but Yoki carefully laid the leaf on my ankle and wrapped the wet towel around it. It was deliciously cool. My hot, achy ankle felt a little better.

Yoki sat opposite me with the fire between us. He tended the fire, patted Noko, kept the towel moist. We waited in silence for morning. Once in a while, his or my stomach would growl loudly, and Noko would whine in commiseration. *Sorry, Noko, for dragging you into this.*

Sometimes the bushes would sway, and a bird's shriek would rend the darkness. The branches of the zelkova, the divine tree, seemed to me to be holding up the ink-black sky.

And that brings us back full circle to the opening of this chapter: "At night in the mountains, I feel a presence," Yoki said quietly.

I wondered if I had ever felt the presence of anything like what he called "a spirit of some kind." I buried my chin in the blanket and tried to think.

But as I stared into the dancing flames, I was overpowered by sleepiness. I always go to bed pretty early. The roughness of the zelkova bark against my back felt super-good, like a back scratcher that reaches all the right places. I was superbly relaxed. Trying to use my brain had an immediate effect: in three seconds, I dozed off.

The next thing I knew, Yoki was changing the towel.

"Sorry," I said. "I must have fallen asleep." I rubbed my eyes and shifted my position. I felt bad, the way you do when someone else is driving and you zonk out in the passenger seat. Not that I would mind one bit if someone went to sleep beside me while I was driving. If Nao, say, fell asleep, I'd be thrilled, thinking how cute she looked and how great it was that I made her feel that safe. Of course, she's never come close to sleeping while I drive. It's as if she thinks dozing off for even a few seconds might spell her doom. Gotta polish my driving skills . . .

Whether it's okay to sleep in the passenger seat or not hasn't got much to do with the night Yoki and I spent on the mountain, so I'll move on. But I want you all to know that I'm not the kind of guy to get upset over such a little thing. Readers, if any of you ever has the opportunity to go on a date with me, feel free to sleep in the passenger seat all you want. If I get sleepy while I'm driving, I'll ask you nicely to pinch me or badmouth me enough to shock me awake.

Crap. Writing all this just makes me feel empty. When I invite Nao out on a drive, two times out of three she turns me down. I'm just putting on airs for you, my imaginary readers.

Where was I? Oh, yeah. Yoki didn't really seem to mind that I'd fallen asleep. Even though he was stuck all night there on the mountain because of me. Maybe he was trying to act broad-minded and tolerant.

No, as much as I hate to admit it, Yoki actually *is* a broad-minded, tolerant guy. Sure, he yells at me a lot, but only when I've been careless at work or made the same mistake yet again, after being told a hundred times. Even in his spats with his wife, most of the time she's the one who starts them. He'll make a retort, but in the end, she gains the upper hand, and he gives in. "That's the secret of a happy marriage," he'll say afterward, and smoke a cigarette out on the veranda, gazing off at the ridge of Mt. Kamusari in the distance, the picture of masculine melancholy.

He pulls off crazy stunts sometimes, but he's basically bighearted. In matters that aren't work related, he doesn't like to have words. Of course, if he ever did go on a rampage, nobody could stop him—he's got superhuman strength. I get the feeling potential adversaries are so cowed, they give him a wide berth.

After he remoistened the towel, Yoki felt my forehead. "Feels like you've got a temperature."

"I do feel a chill."

"That's no good. Wait a minute."

He threw some more branches on the fire, making the flames bigger. He also wrapped his own blanket around me.

"No," I protested. "You'll be cold."

"Nah. I've got Noko." He patted the dog, who was sitting faithfully at his side. "You need to drink some water, too."

"Drink it? Yuck. That's the helmet I always wear."

"So?"

"So dandruff and sweat . . ."

"Think of it as extra nutrition."

Reluctantly I drank the water. To my relief, it tasted normal, not salty. Time had passed since he'd dipped that water from the stream, but it was still cold. Either the temperature on the mountain was dropping, mine was spiking, or the water was so pure it just stayed cold. I don't know.

Getting hydrated made me feel better. My ankle was still hot, and I felt a chill around my shoulders, but I was wide awake now.

Yoki went over by the zelkova, looking for branches to throw on the fire. In the dark, beyond the reach of the firelight, he seemed to have the night vision of a wild animal. I could hear him tramping around, and then he came back by the fire, his arms loaded with branches and leaves.

"What time is it?" I asked.

"Around midnight."

I thought I'd given in to my drowsiness for only ten minutes, but I'd been asleep quite a while, then. The sprain, the fever, and sleeping in the open had taken a greater toll on me than I thought. The night was far from over. I made up my mind to stay awake. After all the trouble I was putting Yoki through, it didn't seem fair for only me to sleep. I knew he must be sleepy, too. But if we both went to sleep and the fire went out, a pre-hibernation brown bear might emerge from the darkness and attack us. The thought terrified me. (Now I can hear Yoki in my ear: *I told* you *there wouldn't be any bears. There are no brown bears in these parts, anyway.*)

More than anything, I wanted to stay awake and talk. It was the perfect chance. I lived in Yoki's house and worked alongside him, but we'd never sat down and had a serious talk. I was shy, for one thing, and

Yoki was so unpredictable I didn't know how to get through to him. But with just the two of us (and Noko) there on the mountain, late at night, I felt like I could talk calmly. I decided to come right out and ask him something that had been on my mind.

"Getting back to what you were saying before, Yoki . . ."

Yoki gave Noko one of the cookies Seiichi had brought and cocked his head inquiringly. "Before?"

"You were saying you felt a familiar presence on the mountain, a kind of spirit."

"Oh, that." He laughed and crunched a cookie. "That was about two hours ago. You must be jet-lagged."

Jet-lagged? I was asleep, not traveling abroad. Also, you've eaten three cookies now and only offered me one. What's up with that?

Shaking off those thoughts, I pushed on. "I've never felt anything like that. When we're working, sometimes I do feel a calm, a stillness. And sometimes I can sense the eyes of monkeys or deer on me." Animals do make their presence felt, although, ever since talking to Iwao about bears when we hiked up Mt. Kamusari in the darkness, I may have gotten a little oversensitive: every movement in the bushes or the treetops gives me goose bumps, as I wonder what dangerous wild beast it might be.

I hated to show weakness to Yoki, but I plowed on. "What you were talking about was something different, though, wasn't it? I've never felt that kind of presence, so maybe that means I'm still a rookie, not a bona fide woodsman."

Is it because I wasn't born in the village? That's what I really wanted to know. When a villager died, his soul flew home, they said, somewhere beyond Mt. Kamusari. Then what about me? If I lived and died here, working in the forest, would I get to be a genuine Kamusari villager? Would my spirit be embraced by the familiar presence Yoki said he felt? The more I thought about it, the more anxious I became. But I couldn't come out and ask in so many words. I'd hate it if Yoki thought I was just feeling down. That's why, even though I had resolved to take the plunge and talk about it, I ended up beating around the bush.

"I dunno." Yoki scratched his jaw. "Maybe it's my imagination, what I feel." For a while he regarded me over the campfire. Then, taking his time, he broke a small branch in two and threw it on the fire. "You haven't lost anybody important to you in the village yet. If I croaked, I bet you'd feel my presence out here. Because my spirit'll go back to Mt. Kamusari." He said that last with a slight smile.

"Don't say that even for fun; it's bad luck. Anyway, you're more likely to outlive me and you know it."

"Yeah, maybe." He grinned and rubbed Noko's head hard.

I smiled back, but inside I was near tears. Yoki had had the sensitivity to pick up on the words I'd swallowed, the question I couldn't get out. My uncertainty over what would happen if I spent my life here and died here. My fear of not being able to see what lay beyond. He'd guessed what I was thinking and offered me reassurance: *One day, you'll be able to feel the presence. You'll have a strong tie to Mt. Kamusari.*

Being tied to something usually feels oppressive. Nobody likes to be tied up or tied down. But I felt a huge sense of relief. Someday, I would be tied to the mountains of Kamusari. The way I was tied to my mother before I was born. I would join the ranks of all who had gone before me. My spirit would linger on the mountain, giving rookie workers like me the heebie-jeebies and filling genius woodsmen like Yoki with peace.

It sounds childish and crazy, but that's what went through my mind. Maybe it was because Yoki and I were the only living souls on the mountain in the deep of night.

I looked up at the interlocking bare branches of the zelkova. A multitude of silver stars hung from them, suspended, like drops of water.

"So you think about death, too," I said.

"Now and then I do, sure."

"Now and then?"

"If you thought about it all the time, you'd go nuts." He was sitting cross-legged, showing no sign of feeling the cold. "But in the mountains, accidents happen. You just never know. I've told Miho that if anything happens to me, she mustn't fall apart."

That took me by surprise. In their constant sparring and making up, he and Miho seemed so full of life—but they made time for serious talk.

"Listen, Yoki," I said. "I heard about the accident twenty years ago."

"Who told you?" Even in the darkness, I could see his expression stiffen.

"Mr. Yamane, but don't blame him. I made him tell me. When I was walking in the graveyard, I couldn't help noticing that an awful lot of people died on the same day. That's why."

He sighed.

"It was a bus accident?"

"Yep. When the news came, I was eating lunch with Granny Shige."

Yoki had been in a bad mood that day. And not only that day. As a fifth grader starting puberty and a rebellious phase, both at the same time, he was constantly on edge for no reason.

His parents had set out for Mt. Omine on May 4, leaving him, their only son, with Granny Shige, who back then was still able to get around.

"If it gets cold at night, put on an extra blanket," his mother said.

"Be good and I'll bring you back a souvenir," his father said.

But Yoki had sulked and never said a proper goodbye. His parents walked off and crossed the bridge, looking back again and again as they went, before boarding the bus at the meeting place. That was the last time Yoki ever saw them alive.

"It still gets to me," he said. "Why'd I let 'em go without even a smile? I dream about that morning a lot, and in my dreams I'm always sulking."

"Your parents must have understood you were at that age."

I could relate. Until pretty recently, I'd been rebellious myself. My parents were always telling me what to do; I thought talking to them was hard and a pain in the ass. Now, maybe because I'm living away from them, or because I've smartened up, I can talk to them a lot more easily. But Yoki hadn't had time to smarten up before his parents were gone forever.

He responded glumly to my clumsy attempt at offering comfort: "Yeah, I guess."

His parents were supposed to get back the evening of the sixth, but an accident on a mountain road in Nara had ended their lives. When the police had phoned with the news, Granny Shige had sunk to the floor, receiver in hand.

"What would it be like, being in an accident like that?" Yoki said. *"Whoosh, kaboom."*

Granny Shige had been so upset that she questioned the police over and over; it took time for her to grasp the situation. "And ever since, she's been hard of hearing." Whether that was the cause of Granny Shige's deafness, I didn't know, but a shock like that could well do it to a person, I thought.

Listening to the words his grandmother spoke into the receiver, Yoki had put two and two together. He jumped up and ran all the way to Seiichi's house. When he rushed in, Seiichi, then in high school, was just setting down the receiver.

"For a second," Yoki told me, "he looked like the ghost of a cucumber. Pale green with shock."

In a steady voice, Seiichi said, "You'll need your wallet and ID. I'll get someone to drive us."

By then, the usually peaceful village was in the throes of despair. People stood in front of their houses and out in the road, trading information—what little there was. The search was impeded because the bus had plunged into a valley. Some people hung their heads in concern, while others sobbed, convulsed with grief. Still others stood in clusters and talked about how to get to the site of the accident. The entire village was in a state of uncertainty and confusion.

In the end, the village office decided to provide vehicles. A collection of vans, sedans, and official cars was scrambled together, and people set off en masse for the scene of the accident. Those who went included relatives and village officials. Old Man Saburo went along as the representative of Kamusari district, driving his own car.

Granny Shige and Yoki rode in the back seat of a van. Yoki was seated next to Seiichi. No one spoke. The atmosphere was tense, and also full of an odd sense of elation. According to Yoki, if somebody had said, "We're on our way to a picnic," the others might have agreed: *Was that it? Yeah, sounds about right.*

In the afternoon light, the May mountains were cloaked in a vibrant, dazzling green. But Yoki felt nothing as he looked out the window. Ordinarily he would have been thinking, *I can't wait to stop wasting time in that stupid school, grow up, and spend my days in the mountains.* Both he and Seiichi had been helping out with forestry work since they were little.

They made several stops along the way so that a village official could call for updates. This was before mobile phones were common, so each time, he had to borrow a phone at a roadside house or shop after explaining the situation.

The microbus hadn't yet been lifted from the valley. No one knew the fate of those on board. The location of the accident was a mountain road, narrow to begin with and crowded now with vehicles connected to the investigation. The van Yoki and the others were in was directed to a nearby village office.

They arrived at the small office while there was still daylight. The workers there were in a flurry, trying to gather information.

As night came on, it grew cold in the little village nestled in the mountains. Yoki and the rest were transferred to the gymnasium of the elementary school, next to the village office, to wait for news. Kind locals provided them with blankets, and the local women, having quickly organized a soup kitchen, offered onigiri and miso soup.

The Kamusari villagers all wore subdued expressions. Even Yoki, as he forced himself to eat, had a bad feeling. Why was the rescue taking so long? Yes, there were a lot of people in their group, but still, why were they all waiting in a gymnasium and not a hospital?

"Yoki, you'd better prepare yourself," Seiichi told him. "This could be really bad."

"No . . ." For once, Yoki said, he had resented Seiichi's calm, collected manner. "It's too soon to tell, isn't it?"

"You mustn't cry," Seiichi told him gently. "If they ask you to identify your parents, can you do it?"

"What do you mean?"

"Granny Shige might collapse. You've got to be strong."

Oh, right, Yoki thought in a trance. *If Mom and Dad are dead, someone has to identify the bodies.* It still didn't feel real, but he looked at Seiichi and nodded.

From the mountains, sunk in darkness, came the sound of a police siren. Unable to sit still, all the Kamusari villagers went out into the schoolyard. The police car was followed by a line of ambulances and fire trucks. There were official-looking black cars, too. All of them were headed toward the elementary school.

As they found out later, the little village didn't have many emergency vehicles, so just as Kamusari had done, they had rounded up vehicles belonging to public facilities. A fleet of cars was needed to transport the bodies brought up from the valley floor.

Several officers emerged from the police cars parked in the schoolyard. One of them told everyone to go back inside, and then he began to explain. He said there was no more hope of finding survivors. The team had recovered all the bodies. These would be brought into the gymnasium, and after undergoing a postmortem by a physician, they would need to be identified by relatives.

Then, for the first time, Yoki noticed an old man with a white lab coat over his shoulders, standing in the officer's shadow. *I bet he's the only doctor in town,* he thought. *Just like Kamusari. Too bad for him, getting called out on a job like this. Anyway, what a shiny, bald head!* Nothing that was happening had felt remotely connected to him, Yoki told me.

Strangely enough, the officer's explanation did not provoke screams or tears. People merely stood around blankly or collapsed onto the floor. Granny Shige crumpled for the second time that day. Yoki quickly crouched down and supported her, as she seemed near fainting.

Bodies wrapped in blankets and gray plastic sheets started to be brought into the gym. The floor seemed suddenly to go soft and squishy, Yoki said. "It felt fluffy, like a cushion, so it was hard to keep your balance. I went over to the rows of bodies, feeling like I might fall."

"I can't have Yoki do such a thing. I'll identify them," Granny Shige had insisted, but her hips and knees wouldn't let her stand.

Some of the victims had been tentatively identified by the names on their possessions. Others had the items of clothing they were wearing listed on a piece of paper attached to the gray sheet. Everyone in Kamusari knew each other so well that a clothing description was enough for them to agree, *This must be So-and-so.*

"It's funny," Yoki told me quietly. "One look at my mother's fingers and I knew it was her. For my old man, it was the sight of his belly. When you're close to someone, you know those little things."

Yoki told the officer, "These are my mother and father." The officer responded, "My condolences," and bowed his head low to Yoki, a ten-year-old child.

Old Man Saburo took Yoki back to Granny Shige's side. When Yoki nodded in confirmation, her face scrunched up, and she sobbed. Old Man Saburo knelt down and comforted her. Sounds of weeping and wailing were beginning to rise all around the gymnasium.

Still in a trance, Yoki went outside. Seiichi, who had identified his parents first, was standing in a corner of the schoolyard. Yoki went up to him and said his name.

Without a word, Seiichi put his arms around Yoki and held him close. Yoki was just entering a growth spurt, and his face came up to Seiichi's chest. The warmth of being held was reassuring, and being with someone he had known all his life gave him the courage to ask: "What'll we do?" He started to tremble. "What'll we do from now on, Seiichi?"

"It's all right," Seiichi said firmly. "You'll go on living down the street from me, and when you grow up, you'll work with me in the forest. Nothing will be different. I guarantee it."

Through Seiichi's white shirt came the sound of his heart beating fast. Yoki understood then that Seiichi, too, was shaken, and yet he was offering him, Yoki, encouragement. He felt grateful. Then, realizing that his father and mother would never again be around to encourage and scold him, he raised his voice and howled in grief like an animal.

A thin, pale moon shone faintly amid the dark, rolling mountains.

Yoki told the story without emotion, but it knocked me over. A fifth grader is still a child. When I was that age, all I thought about was playing with my friends after school. About the only unpleasant part of my life then was attending cram school twice a week. But Yoki had lost his parents in an accident and identified their bodies. Even now, if I had to do that, I'm not sure I'd be capable of it. And here I am an adult, supposedly. Pitiful.

"For a while after that, it was tough." Yoki stirred the fire with his ax handle, and the flames burned brighter. "Other kids besides Seiichi and me lost their parents, too. Some of them went to live with relatives outside the village."

If not for Granny Shige, Yoki might have been forced to leave Kamusari, too. Besides his skills as a woodsman, the other thing he took pride in was his physical strength. If he'd grown up outside Kamusari, he might have gotten lost in the seamy side of life.

I said a quick prayer to the god of Kamusari: *Thanks so much for letting Granny Shige live a long life. You must have decided it wouldn't do to let a wild animal like Yoki run free outside the village.*

"And Seiichi was still a minor, too," I said.

"Yep. He's got tons of relatives, and his parents were loaded. The minute they died, all kinds of relatives and would-be relatives came pouring in."

Seiichi had swiftly safeguarded the mountains and family property through a legal advisor attached to Nakamura Lumber. Miho's parents, who were his distant relatives, became his guardians, and Old Man Saburo took over the business aspects of the company. Those three had continued fending off so-called relatives until Seiichi finished high school and university and could head Nakamura Lumber. Thanks to their efforts, Kamusari maintained its rich legacy of forested mountains.

"What happens is, mountains get divided up among heirs and sold, and pretty soon, with no one to look after the forests, they fall into ruin." Continuing to tend the fire with his ax handle, Yoki sighed. "Of course, up against Seiichi, those relatives and so-called relatives didn't stand a chance. He'd been groomed to take over as master from the time he was little."

"Like a prince trained to be king."

"Maybe not quite that grand. We're talking about Kamusari, after all. But yeah, you could say he was trained to be king of the mountain. After all," he said with a grin, "the mountains are his."

Seiichi, always so calm, so serious about the mountains. Seiichi standing all alone in a rice paddy, paying his respects to the god. Now I understood the universal trust and respect people accorded him as the master. His father must have been the same way.

Together, the people of Kamusari had joined hands to surmount a crisis that blindsided them. So many lives suddenly lost, yet in time the village recovered. Life, it seemed to me, had returned to normal. Nakamura Lumber was managing the forestland, Seiichi had grown into a fine master, and Yoki was full of his old mischief.

"But you know," he said, "I still have nightmares. I hear their voices, my mom and dad. Granny Shige and I are standing in front of the house, seeing them off. I know I'll never see them again, but I go right on sulking. I never say goodbye."

When he had bad dreams, Miho would wake him up, he said. It was always hard to come back to reality, so usually he'd go out on the veranda and smoke a cigarette, looking off at the ridgeline of Mt. Kamusari, where the souls of the dead are said to return.

Suddenly I knew why Yoki had married Miho. Having lost his family so young, he must have wanted a family of his own. But not just anyone would do. It had to be someone who knew firsthand all he had lost, all his pain and sadness. Someone who understood his circumstances and who could, knowing all that, bind him firmly—forcibly, if need be—to the world of the living. There was no one but Miho. She loved Yoki deeply and sought to understand him, and she possessed the passion and brightness of the sun.

"When I'm working deep in the forest, on the mountain," Yoki said, "I feel like I can come as close to the dead as I do in my dreams. Old Man Saburo says mountains are the boundary between this world and the next."

When Yoki was out drinking, maybe he liked to sleep on the bank of the Kamusari River because he wanted to feel a bond. A microbus that fell into a ravine. The soft sound of killifish eggs hatching. Fireflies flitting back and forth. The surface of the river, reflecting swaying pampas grass. Trout under a thin layer of ice, waiting for spring. Water springing from Mt. Kamusari becoming the Kamusari River, flowing from the dead to the living.

Just as Seiichi had done long ago, I wanted to put my arms around Yoki, shake him hard, and tell him, *It's okay!* But of course I didn't. Yoki was way bigger than me, and he had so much stamina he could probably run around the mountains all day and then toss off five hundred squats. If I tried to comfort him, he was likely to scoff: "What are you doin'?"

Instead, I said, "Yoki, get some sleep. I'll watch the fire." I tossed him a blanket and motioned for him to lie down.

"Listen to the big man." His cheeks twitched, as if he were trying not to laugh. "And not so long ago you were going *Eek, a bear!* and falling all over yourself in surprise. And the bear turned out to be Noko!"

"Shut up and go to sleep." I threw a handful of leaves at him.

Holding Noko, Yoki pulled the blanket over himself and lay down. "Wake me up in two hours."

"Okay."

"If a bear comes out, I'll save you."

"All right already."

Soon he was asleep. I was determined to keep watch so I could keep the fire going, and so I could wake up Yoki if he was having a nightmare. The swelling in my ankle seemed to have gone down a little.

The treetops rustled. The sky above was strewn with silent stars. Somewhere, a bird took wing and a small animal scurried by. Noko's triangular ears fluttered like butterfly wings.

Somehow, night on the mountain no longer held terrors for me. A darkness as warm and dense as when I closed my eyes in bed at home surrounded and embraced us. Protecting us. Whispering to us.

Yoki and I traded off once after that, and I slept a little, leaning against the zelkova.

"Wake up!" Yoki yelled.

It was five thirty. The mountain was still pitch-dark.

"What the heck! The sun's not up yet."

Ignoring my protest, Yoki threw ice from the helmet onto the fire. "That's how cold it got. The water froze." He stamped out the fire, careful to make sure it was out. "Time to be off."

I figured he must be starving. There's no reasoning with a hungry beast, so I gave in and tried to stand but couldn't. When I put weight on my ankle, it really hurt. There was no way I could make it down that steep mountainside on my own.

"How about lifting me out of here by helicopter?"

"Forget it. A tree from Mt. Kamusari like that chestnut is worth a small fortune. You, on the other hand, we couldn't sell for a dime."

"Okay, so I'm staying here till my sprain heals?"

"I'll carry you."

"What?"

"On my back." He turned around and squatted down. "Let's go, climb on. Wear your helmet and carry the blankets."

"You can't! I've bulked up. I'm pretty heavy now."

"Not compared to timber."

Yoki insisted, so I got on his back, holding the blankets. I was dubious, but he stood up and started off down the mountain, his footsteps steady. He called to Noko and then he was off like the wind, despite the poor footing. Took me completely by surprise. I was clutching the blankets, so my hands weren't free to grab hold and stabilize myself. I actually leaned backward. Using the muscles I had developed, I fought against the wind and the speed and managed to pull myself upright. I quickly stuffed the blankets between my stomach and Yoki's back and wrapped my arms around his neck so I wouldn't fall off.

Noko tore along beside us, as intrepid as a white wolf.

"If you can run like this in the dark, we didn't need to spend the night on the mountain!" I shouted, struggling to be heard over the wind.

"Didn't know I could do it till I tried!"

At the first gray of dawn, we saw the glimmer of a flashlight ahead.

"Yoki, is that you?" Seiichi was climbing toward us.

"Hey, Seiichi!" Yoki ran past him, then stopped and swung around to face him. Centrifugal force made me almost bite my tongue. I hung on to Yoki for dear life.

We weren't far from the road now. Tucked under Seiichi's arm was a cloth stretcher.

"I was pretty sure you'd be on the move early." Knowing Yoki, Seiichi hadn't waited for dawn. "Just not *this* early. For a minute there I thought a wild boar was charging me."

"I got so hungry, I couldn't wait," said Yoki, sliding me off his back and grabbing my arm to support me. It's pretty hard to stand up straight on a steep slope.

"You ate most of the cookies!" I grumbled, but he paid no attention.

In the end, they decided Yoki's back was safer and more secure than the stretcher, so I went the rest of the way piggyback, too. Noko wagged his tail furiously, as if to say, *I do wish you'd hurry up and put me in the back of the truck and take me home!* He'd only had a cookie or two to eat all this time. He must have been starving, too. *Sorry, Noko. My bad.*

With Yoki's help, I got in the passenger seat. He drove, and we followed Seiichi down the road. When we rounded a curve, all of a sudden the morning sun shone through the windshield. I remember squinting at the glare. The next moment, I was out cold, apparently. Relief at being rescued after our misadventure, hunger, the sprain, sleeping in the open . . . I had reached my limit. That wild ride on Yoki's back, needless to say, was the last straw.

The next thing I knew, I was back in my room—the six-mat room I'd been given in Yoki's house. The familiar feel of my pillow. The comfortable weight of the covers. I must have gone to sleep in the truck. Since Yoki was driving, it didn't really matter. My thoughts spinning, I stared up at the familiar ceiling, and then something wrinkly came into my line of vision. I yelped in surprise.

Granny Shige, who'd been bending over me, was surprised in turn and fell on her rear.

"Oh, it's you, Granny Shige! What's up?"

She rubbed her hip where she'd fallen and knelt on the tatami by my pillow. "You stayed asleep so long I got worried and came to check on you."

"What?" Hurriedly I sat up and looked outside. It was already dusk.

"You've been asleep all day."

"What about Yoki and Seiichi?"

"At work. It's about time they were getting back."

What toughness! Compared to those two, I was a wimp. Downhearted, I threw off my covers—and saw my sprained right ankle, neatly and firmly bandaged. Judging from the smell, under the bandage there was a poultice, too.

"When did that happen?"

"Yoki and Seiichi carried you in here." Granny Shige worked her mouth. "It was a bad sprain, so they phoned for the doctor right away."

There's only one doctor in Kamusari. In hay fever season, I go to him for medicine. He's pretty old and hard of hearing. I have to yell, "It's the pollen! Pollen! My nose is running!" or he's liable to give me an enema pack.

I've heard villagers say, "Going to the doctor tires me out so much, I always come down with something." He'll take someone suffering from hay fever and send them home sick. His clinic is the ultimate in a self-promoting business.

"Nice of him to come."

"Yoki drove him here and back. Miho wound the bandage, and I used a poultice from the medicine chest."

Then why bother calling the old doctor? I wondered.

The wrinkles in her face deepened. I think she was smiling. "I'm glad you woke up. Miho was worried, too. She went out shopping just now. I told Yoki to bring back some more loquat leaves, so after supper I'll make you some medicine."

"Thank you." I tried to get up and walk, but it still hurt too much. I hopped across the room.

"Where are you going? You have to pee?"

"No. Work. They're out by Hyoroku Marsh today, I think." I figured I could at least help with the work site cleanup.

"No, you don't!"

She grabbed my good ankle to stop me, and I lost my balance and came near to crashing onto the tatami face-first. I braced myself with my arms, as if doing push-ups, and managed to avert disaster. On my hands and knees, I twisted around to face her in protest. "Granny Shige! What are you trying to do to me?" I could have gotten really hurt, worse than a sprain.

"You've got to spend the next few days at home, resting."

"Is that what the doctor said?"

She shook her head solemnly. "I know more about injuries and sickness than that quack ever will. Sprain your ankle once and it's likely to happen again, so don't make light of it. The best thing you can do is stay quiet and rest your foot."

Yeah, but . . . I was still little better than a trainee on the job, so the workload wasn't as bad as it might have been, and staying home and doing nothing would bore me silly. There was no entertainment to speak of in the village. Sitting around the house all day would be excruciating. But Granny Shige kept looking at me with a penetrating gleam in her eyes, summoning her full dignity, so I had no choice but to consent. She's just as strong-willed as you'd expect. After all, she raised Yoki, that wild animal, single-handed.

Come to think of it, Granny Shige lost a son and a daughter-in-law in the accident. She's seen more than her share of trouble and sorrow, but you'd never know it to look at her, sitting quietly like a bean-jam bun the way she does.

Back on the futon, flat on my back, I groaned, "How could I be so dumb and end up like this!"

"What do you mean?" Granny Shige worked her mouth and cocked her head, puzzled. "You get to take time off work like a big shot for once. What's wrong with that?"

"It's boring. I'd rather be out on the mountains."

She chuckled. "Well, you've changed, haven't you? In the beginning you were always complaining: *High places are scary! Leeches sucked my blood!*"

"You've got too good a memory for such an old lady."

She chuckled again. "I'm only saying, you've made yourself into quite a worker. And that's not all." She leaned over me. "Even if you can't go into the mountains, there are lots of interesting things to know about right here in the village."

"Like what?" I sat up, expecting another folktale. "By the way, you know that story you told about the snake god? I wrote it down."

"I knew you were sitting at the desk at night. Are you keeping a diary, Yuki?"

"A diary? Hmm. More like . . . notes and memoranda," I said with a touch of importance, watching for her reaction. She nodded with apparent interest.

I'd kept this record private until then, but I decided showing it to Granny Shige might be okay. Having even one reader would motivate me. I impressed upon her that it was a secret and turned on the computer. It made its usual start-up sound. It's an old model, so it takes a long time to boot up. Granny Shige seemed to confuse the computer with a TV set. She knelt on the floor beside me and stared at the screen doubtfully. "Where's the remote control? There's no picture." It tickled me.

Finally, the computer was ready, and I opened a file. It told about the snake god, and my drives with Nao, and all kinds of village happenings.

"Goodness! A computer is something, isn't it? Just look at all those sentences it holds! You wrote all this, Yuki?"

"I did."

"Aren't you a wonder! I can't even bring myself to write a proper letter."

It was nice having Granny Shige praise me. I felt a little proud. "Finding stuff to write about isn't always easy. If you hear anything else interesting, be sure and let me know."

"Come with me a minute."

Granny Shige put her hands on her thighs and slowly got to her feet. Then she hobbled toward the veranda, supporting herself with the wall. Ordinarily I would have gone along at her side, but my ankle couldn't support my own weight. *First you tell me to rest, and now you want me to move around?* I hopped along behind her. With every hop, my right ankle, suspended in air, sent a jolt of pain to my brain.

Granny quietly pulled back the curtain on the veranda and pointed outside. Mr. Yamane was wandering up and down the road, eyes on the ground. He didn't notice us spying on him.

"What's he doing?"

"Looking for something, so he says."

"Looking for what?"

Granny laughed. "Been like that since last night."

"Is that what's interesting?"

"If the weather's good tomorrow, come sit outside here and wait for him to show up." Her voice fell to a whisper. "When he goes by, ask him, 'Lost something, did you? Got your *o-age* ready?'"

I had no idea what that might mean. Granny Shige saw my confusion and grinned, her eyes crinkling into crescent shapes, like a fox's.

Miho came back from shopping just then, so I didn't pursue it. Anyway, peeps, what do you think was so interesting? I'll report back later!

The next day, when I said those words to Mr. Yamane, exactly as Granny Shige had told me to, it caused a bit of an uproar. Granny Shige's sly—she likes to play tricks.

Then Yoki came back from work, and we all sat around the low table for supper. While putting away his three bowlfuls of rice, he teased me about my ankles: "They're weak. You've got the ankles of an octopus." He really gets on my nerves.

But I'm glad Yoki and I got to talk on the mountain that night. Day after day, he lives with Miho, Granny Shige, and me, eating, laughing, going to work, and sleeping, while on the Buddhist altar, his mother and father smile on. I'm pretty sure that's all he needs. As a kid, he had an experience more painful and tragic than I can imagine, but he didn't succumb. In the end, he got back everything important, everything he wanted. All while swinging his ax and earning his living on the mountains, continuing his daily routines.

And that's how Yoki's and my mountain mishap came to an end.

5

THE FIFTH NIGHT

LOST AND FOUND IN KAMUSARI

How goeth it, everyone?

No, that doesn't sound right. I thought it would be cool to write in old-fashioned samurai style, but after just one sentence I'm giving up.

This record has been my little secret from the beginning, but the other day I told Granny Shige about it. I was hoping she'd share village legends and gossip I could write about, but I think I messed up. Now every time we're alone in the house, she comes up and asks conspiratorially, "How's the writing coming, Yuki?" My job keeps me busy enough, and in between I have to find time to ask Nao out on dates, too. It's not like I write every day. So I tell her, "Not much progress." But she won't let it go.

"You know Ooka Echizen and Toyama no Kin-san?" she'll say. "I want to read stories like those."

Oh sure. The legendary samurai heroes on TV. No pressure.

"Granny Shige," I said once, trying to change the subject, "you watch a lot of samurai reruns on TV. Are they interesting?"

She nodded. "*Mito Komon* is good, but if you ask me, Mito spends too much time on the road. Wherever he goes, he finds wrongdoing, which only shows you how twisted people's hearts are. He needs to quit traveling, settle down, and run the country like it should be run."

So much for the venerable vice-shogun of the land, traveling incognito, dispensing justice and restoring peace wherever he goes.

Granny Shige generally speaks her mind. A lot of the time she sits quietly, working her mouth, so you can't tell if she's awake or asleep, but when she's watching the news, a change comes over her. If she hears a politician's secretary was arrested in connection with a bribery case, she'll tsk-tsk reproachfully, "For shame." If she hears a schoolteacher committed an indecent act with a minor, she'll snort, "The damn fool." She shakes her head as if the world were coming to an end. And then she always adds sternly, "Yoki, you better watch yourself, too!"

If it's a case of bribery that's got her upset, Yoki'll say, "If only somebody *would* try to slip me a little something! Let 'em, I say!" But when it's an indecent act with a minor that's got Granny riled, Yoki can't help himself. He'll say in all seriousness, "Not me. I don't rob the cradle." Then Miho, who's been munching on a slice of pickled radish, gets a wicked gleam in her eyes.

"What's *that* supposed to mean? You like a woman who's older and more experienced, is that it? I'm not all that experienced, myself, so tell me: just who is this playmate you have in mind? Out with it!"

Then they're back at it again, as usual. I can only sigh and wish Mito Komon and his retinue would stop by our place for once and restore peace.

Anyway, since Granny Shige is my only actual reader, I'd like to respond to her request. That's why I started out trying to sound like an old-time samurai, but it's beyond me. Anyway, Kamusari doesn't have any need for Tokugawa-style justice. There are no sneaky thieves here, and I bet there's never been a single murder, either.

So yeah, Kamusari is as peaceful as can be, and yet, of course, nobody's life is totally free of hassles. The village has seen its share of trouble, from disputes over water rights to complaints that "the young man next door slept with my wife" (seems like in every age, there are guys like Yoki who can't keep it in their pants). Historically, when things like that happened, the villagers didn't turn to a samurai hero like Ooka Echizen or Toyama no Kin-san. They turned to Inari, the fox deity of harvest and rice.

On the mountain behind Iwao's house is a small shrine dedicated to Inari, who Granny Shige says can't abide dishonesty. When two people embroiled in a dispute tell different stories, and the villagers can't tell which one's telling the truth, they go to the shrine, offer o-age (more commonly known as *abura-age*, deep-fried tofu that foxes are said to love), and state their cases publicly. Within a week or so, one of them is guaranteed to have an accident or come down with a fever, proving that they were conveniently distorting the truth. Inari sees through lies and metes out punishments accordingly.

I know what you're thinking: *More Kamusari fantasy!* When Granny Shige first told me all this, I thought so, too. But today the villagers take a modern approach. To prevent disagreements over water rights, they use pumps and little sluice gates to irrigate all the paddies with water from the Kamusari River. And since the villagers' average age is around sixty, I've never heard of any scandals involving infidelity. (Yoki is a special case, but lately even he's been behaving himself.)

Yet even now, the villagers hold Inari in great reverence. Every March, there's an event at the shrine called *mochimaki* where *mochi*, rice cakes, are thrown into a crowd for people to catch. I didn't know about it this year because I was working, but apparently the village women always go there to get mochi. Now that I think of it, I remember a time in the spring when Miho was making dishes I associate with New

Year's: *zoni* soup and *kinako* mochi, rice cakes dusted with sweetened soybean flour.

The villagers really go in for mochi. There's even a mochimaki telephone chain. Whenever a new house is built, at the ridgepole-raising ceremony it's traditional for the owner to host a mochimaki. People spread the word via telephone. Then when the day comes, the whole village shows up (especially women), bustling and eager. Miho has a special cloth bag she uses on those occasions. "I grab them in both hands and stuff them in the bag, as many as I can get my hands on," she says. How much mochi can one person eat?

When Seiichi got married, he took the opportunity to repair the roof of his house. It's unusual to host a mochimaki just for house renovations, but he is the master, after all. He put on a grand event for the villagers, one they still talk about. They used up an entire straw bag of rice—sixty kilos' worth! How much mochi can one village eat?

But mochi wasn't the point. I was talking about the god Inari.

There aren't too many cases today where Inari is called on to hand down a formal judgment, but he does have power to help people find lost objects, they say. People who've lost or mislaid something go to the shrine, and in a week or so, the missing item pops up.

My initial reaction on hearing this was *another Kamusari fantasy!* but there does seem to be something to it. I was amazed to learn that people from outside the village drive here just to ask Inari's help. There's no shrine priest or shrine office, mind you, just a tiny little shrine clinging to the side of the mountain.

So this time I'll tell a tale about searching for lost objects. Remember what I wrote last time, about Mr. Yamane wandering around in the road? That was before I knew anything about the shrine. Completely in the dark, I just went up to him the next day and repeated what Granny Shige had told me to say.

All that morning I sat on the veranda, waiting for Mr. Yamane to go by. The swelling in my ankle was starting to subside. Maybe Granny Shige's loquat concoction was working. My fever was down, too, but I still couldn't walk normally. Unable to go to work, I was bored.

Yoki and Noko had gone into the mountains, and Granny Shige was at eldercare in Hisai. The eldercare center has a nice big bath and friends she can pass the day with, so she enjoys her twice-weekly trips there. Usually someone comes to the house to pick her up, but that day Miho had errands in town, so she drove Granny Shige to the center in her little red car.

I was sprawled on the veranda in a lazy mood. Soft winter sunshine shone through the glass doors. Even without the kerosene stove on, the veranda with its southern exposure was as toasty as a little greenhouse. Looking out at the garden and the line of mountains in the distance, I dozed through the morning. I'd intended to keep an eye out for Mr. Yamane, but I must have still been tired out from my little misadventure on South Mountain.

At noon I heated up the pork stew and fried egg Miho had left for me and ate a solitary lunch. It occurred to me that until then, I'd always eaten with other people. In Kamusari I ate breakfast and supper with Yoki and his family, gathered around the little round table, and lunch with my team in the mountains. Back at school in Yokohama, I used to eat my bento or the school lunch with my friends, and at home Mom was always around. For a while after coming here, I thought she was a horrible mother, packing me off here to work without giving me any choice in the matter, but looking back, she wasn't so bad after all.

When you eat alone, you're done in about five minutes. I turned on the TV, but that only accentuated the silence in the room and made me more uncomfortable. Yours truly grew up pretty spoiled, it appears.

I went back to the veranda, and this time I stayed awake and watched the road. Neighbors would happen by, see me encamped there, and nod hello. I nodded back. No need to worry that they'd look down their noses at me for lounging around and not getting things done. Word travels fast in the village. Everybody knew all about my sprain. Yoki must've told the story, adding humorous flourishes at my expense, no doubt. Grr.

There was no sign of Mr. Yamane. Finally I realized this was a weekday, so he must be working somewhere in the mountains. Just as I was about to give up, along he came. Like the day before, he was walking with his eyes on the ground. Was he taking the day off? He rambled along with no apparent destination in mind, peering into the ditch at the side of the road. It was all very strange.

I opened the veranda door and called, "Mr. Yamane!" I started to get up, but my ankle protested. I couldn't get up without a cane.

Mr. Yamane looked up and glanced around. I waved to catch his eye, and he came hurrying over, crossing through the front yard.

"You injured your leg. Don't stand up."

He's blunt but well-meaning. He sat down beside me.

"You took the day off?" I asked. In return, I got a sigh. He hung his head and stared at his knees. Again, he means well, but he's just not very sociable. I remembered Granny Shige's advice and asked a different question. "You lost something, did you? Have you got some o-age ready?"

The words meant nothing to me, but their effect on Mr. Yamane was electric. He all but grabbed me and said in excitement, "So you think there's nothing left but to go to the shrine?"

"Um, shrine?"

"You mean you said that without knowing what it means?"

"Sorry. Granny Shige said you're searching for something. What did you lose?"

"The devil stinger," he said, lowering his voice.

"What? That dried fish?"

"*Dried fish?* That's the guardian deity of those who work in the forest, I'll have you know."

I had aggravated him. I apologized again.

He sighed and looked up at the sky. "I must be cursed. How could I have lost it? I guess my luck's run out."

Working in forestry has its dangers, and many people become superstitious. Iwao is a prime example. That episode long ago with the zelkova must have really left its mark. Every morning before setting off for work, he stands before Mt. Kamusari with his palms pressed together, and once every three months or so he'll take the day off, saying he just doesn't feel right about going in that day. Seiichi doesn't mind. "It's important to respect that gut feeling," he says. Better to take the day off than force yourself to go to work when your heart isn't in it and end up getting injured.

Seiichi and Old Man Saburo have their superstitious sides, too. Whenever they come upon a giant tree, they always offer it water or tea. Yoki is the least superstitious of the lot, but even he taps a tree trunk twice before cutting it down. He does it out of respect for the god of the mountain, they say.

After his harrowing experience at last year's grand festival, Mr. Yamane took to carrying around the devil stinger as protection, but now his good luck charm was missing. I could see why he might think he was cursed.

"How long has it been missing?"

"Since the day you and Yoki got stuck on the mountain. So if it was stolen, you and he are in the clear."

Thanks a lot. Even if I had the chance, I'd never be tempted to pinch your creepy dried fish.

On the day of the incident (?), he'd attended a village assembly. About ten people got together from the three village districts—Shimo, Naka, and Kamusari—to conduct a postmortem on this year's

Oyamazumi festival. They drank tea and ate snacks while they talked, and the meeting broke up around three.

Mr. Yamane was one of the representatives of Kamusari district. The festival happens every year, so there wasn't much to discuss. There was a report on expenses, and they drew lots to see which district would write up the minutes. Everything went smoothly. In the end, everything they decided would be reported to Seiichi.

At the assembly, Mr. Yamane had boasted about his devil stinger; its presence, he said, accounted for the success of this year's festival. They should all be grateful. He took it out of his jacket pocket and showed it to everyone. One after another, they had handled it, looked it over, and commented: "This is amazing!" "Be sure and take good care of it!" Mr. Yamane was in such good spirits he drank too much tea and twice got up to go to the bathroom. Then the meeting was adjourned, and he left in a rush.

"I just can't remember whether I had the devil stinger in my pocket then or not," he said. He'd needed to call the lumberyard by five o'clock about something or other, and that errand had been uppermost in his mind. From the assembly hall to his house was a short walk of less than five minutes. He went home and made the call, and only then did he realize the devil stinger was gone.

"I hurried back to the assembly hall, but it wasn't there. I thought at first one of them might have made off with it, but nobody in the village would do anything that outrageous. So I must have dropped it along the way. I've been hunting for it here ever since."

I shivered. Being from outside the village, I sure as heck didn't want to come under suspicion. Just as he'd said, the day the devil stinger went missing, everybody in the Nakamura team had been on South Mountain minding our own business, making sure the chestnut log got safely off.

"Maybe a cat or something found it lying in the road and carried it off," I said. "It does look a little like smoked bonito."

"It's a guardian deity, I told you! Smoked bonito? That's sacrilege."

Not even a cat would come near your devil stinger. But if I said that, he'd only get madder, so I kept my mouth shut.

Somebody must have taken it. That was all I could think. The likeliest suspects were the other participants in the assembly. They'd had opportunity and motive, since after hearing Mr. Yamane praise the thing to the skies, they knew it was valuable. I cautiously suggested this.

"Don't be a fool," he said. "I know them all. Not one of them would take another man's property. By your logic, I'd have to suspect you."

"M-me? Why?"

"After you learned about the devil stinger during the festival, you could have decided you wanted it. Then you saw it lying in the road by your house and thought, *It's mine! Heh, heh.*"

"Now wait just a minute." My voice was shrill. "I sprained my ankle, and I can hardly walk. Ever since they carried me home yesterday morning, I haven't set foot outside this house."

"I know. I was just funning you." He said this with a straight face. I couldn't tell if he believed me or not.

Then another scary thought entered my mind. "But in that case, maybe Granny Shige . . ."

"What's that old granny got to do with it?"

Hesitantly, I told him my idea. "She seemed to know exactly what you were looking for. And she, of all people, would understand how valuable it is. Couldn't she have found it and pocketed it?"

"Too old. She can barely walk. Doesn't go out of the house by herself, does she?"

No, I had to admit, but I'd seen her move with surprising swiftness and agility. I've sometimes wondered if her difficulty walking isn't all an act.

As I stammered, Mr. Yamane laughed for once. "I'm the one who told her, *I lost the devil stinger, so if you catch sight of it, be sure and let me know.* That's why she knew what I was looking for."

Well, that was a relief. It was good to know that no one I was that close to could be the culprit.

"Just about everybody in the village knows the meaning of the devil stinger. If they saw it in the road, they'd bring it to me right away."

I felt a chill. Mr. Yamane seemed to believe in the innate goodness of his neighbors, but you could just as easily take the opposite view and assume all the villagers were suspect. If everybody knew how valuable the devil stinger was, then anybody who found it, whether in the assembly hall or by the wayside, would have motive to filch it.

Yes, the Nakamura team had an alibi for the time when the meeting was held. But what if the devil stinger had fallen in the road instead? Suppose Yoki, just back from our night on the mountain, stumbled on it and thought, *Well, lookee here! Must be my lucky day.* I wouldn't put it past him.

The ballooning number of suspects gave me a headache. Beside me, Mr. Yamane seemed to be devising some sort of plan. He was a guest in the house, and I felt like I owed him at least a cup of tea. But if I went from here to the kitchen and back, I could hear him saying, *So you can walk! It was you after all!*

He suddenly stood up with purpose. "There's nothing for it now but to go see O-Inari-san."

"O-Inari-san?" I repeated blankly. It took my brain a second to register that he meant the fox deity and not the snack food with the same name—those pouches of deep-fried tofu filled with sushi rice and vegetables. They must be named after the fox deity.

"Yes." He looked down at me as I gazed up at him stupidly, and nodded. "You come, too, Yuki."

Despite my throbbing ankle, Mr. Yamane dragged me off with him by force. (Whatever happened to *Don't stand up?*) I borrowed Granny Shige's cane and managed to hobble across the yard and out to the road, while he went and got his pickup. He'd taken the day off, he said, because with the devil stinger unaccounted for, he didn't feel right going into the mountains.

Once I was settled in the passenger seat, Mr. Yamane started the car. First he stopped at the little store by the bridge and bought a pack of deep-fried tofu. I stayed in the car, mystified. He set the purchase in my lap and drove on. We followed the river upstream. There were a few houses along the way, but soon the number trickled down to none at all. Next, we crossed another little bridge and went past Iwao's house, straight up an unpaved road. Mr. Yamane finally pulled up at the foot of a little round mountain. I got out with difficulty, relying on the cane.

With the pack of deep-fried tofu in hand, Mr. Yamane started up a narrow, gently sloping path. I had no idea what was going on, but I hobbled after him, doing my best to keep up. Tree branches formed a canopy overhead. The place was dim and damp and chilly; I could see my breath. It was perfectly still. The sun hadn't set, but there were no birdcalls. The only sound was the constant murmur from a rivulet on the right that fed into the Kamusari River.

It was a little scary. Mr. Yamane's broad, solid back up ahead was a reassuring sight. Though he was the one who'd brought me to this weird place . . .

The pain in my ankle slowed me down, but even so, in less than five minutes I spotted a small wooden torii up ahead. It must have been painted red once, but the paint had all peeled off. The wood was crumbling and the posts were tilting. Beyond it was a dilapidated shrine with double lattice doors, guarded on either side by a stone image of a fox. One had a ball in its mouth, the other a scroll. The foxes were kind of round and plump, like the mountain itself; they made me smile.

Who knew there was a shrine to Inari in a place like this? While I was looking around, Mr. Yamane threw a coin in the collection box in front of the lattice doors. (The box, I might add, was shabby, about the size of a piggy bank.) He took the deep-fried tofu out of the packaging and laid it on a small white dish next to the collection box. Then he rang the bell hanging from the shrine, long and loud. The pull rope was so faded and ratty, I was afraid it might come off.

He clapped twice, bowed his head, and began to pray: "O-Inari-san, O-Inari-san. My devil stinger has disappeared. Please bring it back. I beg of you."

He was the first person I ever saw pray out loud at a shrine. I stood there staring, and when he was done, he turned around.

"Did you hear that, Yuki?" he said in a stern tone.

"Yes."

"Now you go."

Why me? I thought. But, yielding to his determination, I pressed my hands together in front of the mysterious shrine.

"Speak up, now, or O-Inari-san won't hear you."

I'd come this far, might as well go whole hog. "O-Inari-san, O-Inari-san. Please make Mr. Yamane's wish come true. Please!"

He grunted in satisfaction. Why was this grown man dragging me into his world of fantasy? Really, sometimes Kamusari villagers are beyond me.

As we left the shrine, Mr. Yamane looked triumphant, while I tottered behind, leaning on Granny Shige's cane. We went back down the path, and just as we were approaching the pickup, Iwao, home from work, came out the back door of his house.

"Hey there, Yuki!" He smiled and waved. "What are you doing here? Is your ankle better now? Heard you had a rough time."

Yes, my mishap on South Mountain was tough, but so is being dragged around by Mr. Yamane. The verb should be present progressive, I thought, remembering my English grammar: *I am having a rough time.*

Iwao noticed Mr. Yamane over by the pickup and said hello. "You're here with Yuki? Did you two pay a visit to the shrine?"

"We did."

"What did you lose?"

"My devil stinger."

"No! That's terrible." Iwao then came over and patted me on the shoulder. "Yuki, you served as witness. Good for you."

All I did was stand there like a dummy. Seeing my confusion, Iwao and Mr. Yamane took turns explaining.

"When someone goes to the shrine to report a lost object, someone else always has to go along as witness," said Iwao.

"It's that person's job to hear what was lost and what prayer was made," said Mr. Yamane.

Okay, sure. Whatever. At the time, I didn't know the first thing about Inari. That evening, Granny Shige told me the legends and traditions associated with him. Since he despises deceit, I guess the witness is needed to keep people from making self-serving, dishonest requests.

"Yamane, you did everything by the book," said Iwao. "O-Inari-san is sure to find your devil stinger." His voice was strong and confident.

Iwao is famous for his piety (or should I say superstitiousness?), but I couldn't help feeling skeptical. After gobbling up the tofu, the foxes would be so full they wouldn't give a hoot about a dried-up devil stinger. But Mr. Yamane looked pleased, so I just nodded vaguely.

We said goodbye, and Mr. Yamane drove me home. Everyone was back, and Miho was getting supper on. To my amazement, they all knew exactly where I'd been and why. Iwao must have phoned them, but it had happened so fast it seemed like telepathy.

Miho scolded me. "You went off and left the house unguarded, and what if it takes your ankle longer to heal now? What were you thinking?"

Left the house unguarded? Surely there's no need to watch the house. Nobody here locks the door when they go out. That's what I thought, but of course I didn't say so. I apologized.

119

Yoki laughed. "Lost his devil stinger? All he needs to do is dry out another one. He can't see the obvious."

In the end, it really *was* just a dried fish, wasn't it? Yet somehow I didn't want people thinking Yoki and I shared the same sensibility.

All through supper, Granny Shige filled me in about Inari, as I said. Unlike lunch that day, everything tasted delicious, though whether it was because we were all gathered around the little table or because my ankle hurt less, I don't know.

Yoki heated up the bath, and after a good soak I had my bandage and poultice changed and went to bed. Knowing I'd be able to go back to work in the morning, I was as excited as a kid the night before a school field trip.

By the next day, it was common knowledge in the village that Mr. Yamane and I had paid a visit to the shrine together. *Jeez*, I thought, *don't people have anything else to talk about?*

And—hold on to your hats, everybody!—the devil stinger turned up. Two days after we hiked up to the shrine, Mr. Yamane woke up, opened the curtains, and found it lying there on his veranda. It was wet with dew and even more rock-hard than before, maybe from the cold. But it was his devil stinger, beyond a doubt. O-Inari-san must have brought it in the night, he said, overjoyed. He bought two packs of deep-fried tofu and took them to the shrine in thanks.

When I heard the news, I got all excited. *Way to go, O-Inari-san!* I wondered if a fox had found the devil stinger somewhere and taken it to Mr. Yamane. I actually envisioned a scene like that, straight out of a Japanese folktale. I'd been skeptical, but Inari's power turned out to be real.

It was Saturday, so I borrowed Yoki's pickup and went to see Nao. My ankle was finally healed, and I wanted to invite her out for a drive for the first time in a while. I had so many things to tell her.

I opened the front door and called, "Hello. It's Yuki Hirano."

She came right to the door, but she looked kind of down.

"What's wrong? Aren't you feeling good?"

"No, that's not it. The place is a mess, but come on in."

I followed her into the living room and did a double take. She wasn't kidding—the place was a gosh-awful mess. An avalanche of newspapers and other papers covered the tatami. The door to the next room was ajar, and I could see that every drawer in her chest of drawers was open, with clothes spilling out. Her desktop was littered with accessories and writing things. The last time I came, everything had been so tidy. What could have happened?

"Did a burglar come?"

"No."

Her voice was listless. She brought out a teacup from underneath some newspapers. "I've been looking for something since last night, but I can't find it. I just have no idea where it went."

So while I drank the tea she made with a tea bag, I told her all about Mr. Yamane and his lost-and-found devil stinger. All about O-Inari-san and his amazing power to find lost items. She hadn't heard about the recovery of the devil stinger and was unaware of the existence of the little shrine. We live in the same village, but while she teaches school, I work in the mountains. Our worlds, the culture we share and the people we know, are different in scope. Also, she isn't from Kamusari. She's far more used to the village than I am, but news and gossip might not get to her as easily. In this case, the villagers had good reason to hold back. If they'd gone up to her and said, *Thanks to O-Inari-san, a dried devil stinger turned up!* she'd have been seriously confused.

She listened intently, and then nodded as if she'd made up her mind. "Take me there."

"Okay. What'd you lose?"

"A fountain pen." She looked embarrassed. "Seiichi gave it to me when I got hired at the school. I'm always so careful with it, but it just vanished."

Shion Miura

Damn. I was deflated, but I didn't let it show. After going on about the surefire efficacy of Inari, what was I going to do? Tell her, *Maybe it's just as well if that pen of yours doesn't turn up?* Impossible.

But really—after all I'd done to let her know how much I liked her, how could she look me in the face and go on about Seiichi? Who does that? Telling me how she's "always so careful" with his gift—sheesh. *Yeah, I get it. Unlike him, I make peanuts. And I've never given you a present.* I felt lousy.

Maybe Nao was just plain mean. Maybe she'd brought up Seiichi's name on purpose to fan the flames of my jealousy. Then to hell with her!

But I was too far gone on her to go that route. I helped her into the truck and drove in silence. She held on to the deep-fried tofu she'd taken from her fridge and stared out the window as the scenery flew by.

"I've hardly ever been this far into Kamusari district," she said.

"Huh."

"I didn't even know there was an Inari shrine."

"I see."

My answers were so abrupt, she must have sensed something was off. She looked at me inquiringly, but I played dumb. And she didn't say anything else for the rest of the ride.

I panicked a little. Maybe I'd made her mad. What should I do? But I was always the one to give in; that's why she couldn't forget Seiichi. For once, I needed to act manly in front of her. It half killed me to do it, but I stayed taciturn and moody until I parked at the foot of the mountain.

"This way." I walked ahead of her up the narrow pathway. That day, too, it was dim and, because of the rivulet, damp.

"There could be snakes here," she said, sounding so forlorn that I gave up my resolution to stay silent.

"Now that you mention it, they say pit vipers attack the person walking second in line."

Something struck me on the back. My first thought was that I'd been hit by a pit viper. But of course, it was Nao. She'd grabbed hold

122

of my jacket and was yanking me back. "Change places with me!" she begged.

"Gah, you're choking me . . . Come on, Nao, calm down. By now, pit vipers are hibernating."

"Really?" Gradually her grip relaxed.

"Yes. I just said it to tease you. Sorry."

"You're terrible."

She was angry, but even so, she kept clinging to me as we walked toward the shrine. *So Nao's afraid of snakes. Aha.* Feeling her warmth, I started to enjoy the moment. *No, no! You're supposed to stay distant!* I scolded myself. *Don't be such a pushover.*

When we arrived, Nao followed all the steps, just as I described. She made a coin offering, placed the deep-fried tofu on the plate, and rang the bell. (The deep-fried tofu Mr. Yamane had brought the other day was gone. Maybe the foxes really did eat it?)

"I lost a fountain pen that's important to me. Please help me find it, I beg of you." She prayed out loud and then stood there with her palms pressed together and her eyes closed. *If I went missing, I bet she wouldn't pray this hard for me to be found. Come to think of it, she hasn't said anything about my little accident. Does she even know?* I was so inflamed with jealousy, I could hardly stand still.

Afterward we went back to the truck. If Iwao saw us, he'd be sure to tease us. I braced myself, but he must have gone out somewhere with his wife. His back door stayed shut.

Seated in the truck again, Nao neatly folded the empty wrapper and tied it up like an old love letter. I wanted to get going, but she kept gazing off through the windshield at the mountain.

Finally I said, "Nao, seat belt."

"Oh, right." She came to herself and fastened her seat belt.

I turned on the engine and stepped on the gas. "Shall we stop somewhere on the way back? Or would you rather go right home? If you want, I can help you clean up." It was useless. I couldn't keep acting distant with her. But she didn't seem to hear.

She said, "You were mad about something before, weren't you?"

"Who, me?" I smiled at her. "No, I'm not mad."

"Liar. You got all huffy for some reason. I don't get it. What was the matter?"

How cruel can you be, asking me to say the reason out loud! Have mercy, Nao. To change the subject, I said cheerfully, "When's the last time you saw your fountain pen, anyway?"

She seemed dissatisfied, but she said, "Day before yesterday. I had a terrible toothache."

"From a cavity?"

"Yeah. I'm always telling the children to brush their teeth, and then I go and get a cavity. Some example I set."

She called the dentist and made an appointment, and after school she got on her motorcycle and rode to Hisai. Before leaving, she'd grabbed the pen from her desk and put it in her briefcase.

"That's the last time I saw it. Usually when I go home, I take it out and put it on my desk, first thing. Yesterday morning, when I was about to leave for school, I looked in the pen tray, and it wasn't there. I turned my briefcase inside out, but it wasn't there, either. I must have dropped it somewhere."

She phoned the dentist on her break to check if she'd left it there, and she checked all around her desk in the teachers' room, with no luck. Then, starting the night before, she'd turned her house upside down. It amazed me to think she could tear the place apart so thoroughly in such a short time. What power, what passion!

As I listened, I tried to think what I would have done in her place, running a simulation in my mind. Habits are usually unconscious, hard to break. If she'd put the pen in her briefcase, then probably she had taken it out right away, as usual.

"I know! When you went to the dentist, did you take your insurance card?"

"Yes."

"Did you look in the place where you usually keep it? Maybe, when you came back, you put the fountain pen away with the insurance card by mistake."

"You know, I bet I did." Her face brightened. "Go faster! Hurry, hurry!"

Though she was rushing me, I stayed within the speed limit as I drove along Kamusari River. When we got to her house, she burst out of the truck, slid open the front door with almost enough force to break it, and ran inside.

Evening was coming on. I couldn't barge in uninvited; she wouldn't like it, and neighbors' eyes were unforgiving. I peered nervously inside. I heard sounds of slamming and banging, and then she crowed, "Found it!"

She came dashing out, waving the fountain pen in her right hand. "It was right where you said it would be, in the safe with my insurance card!"

In her excitement, she hugged me. I laid my hands gently on her shoulders and put a bit of distance between us. If we were pressed too tightly together, the neighbors' eyes, not to mention a certain part of my body, could spell trouble.

The pen she held tight was dark green. Just the right color for her. Realizing that Seiichi had chosen it for her, once again I felt jealousy threaten to erupt through the top of my head.

She looked up at me, deliriously happy. "Thank you, Yuki. I owe it all to you."

Wow. Hearing her say my name practically made steam come out of my ears. I felt dizzy, but I tried my best to play the part of a silent, stoic man. "I didn't do anything. You owe it all to O-Inari-san." Somehow talking about O-Inari-san didn't fit my image of a silent, stoic man, but I let that pass. "Shall I help you straighten up?"

"No, I'll do it. Thank you so much, really. Bye now."

Gracefully dismissed, I trudged back to the pickup. Only when I started to get in the driver's seat did I realize that she was right behind me.

"Whoa. Sneaking up on me? What for?"

"I couldn't bring myself to call out." She was smiling, still holding the fountain pen. "Before, by any chance, were you jealous?"

How could she come right out and say it to my face like that? I wished she would have a little respect for my desire to leave with my dignity as a man intact.

"What if I was?"

"To be so kind to me right while you were so jealous . . . I mean, what a good kid you are."

I bristled. *A kid, am I? Just because I'm younger than you, don't underestimate me.* With a slight, sardonic smile (okay, it's possible I just looked stiff), I said, "I'm not one of your pupils."

She kept the upper hand without missing a beat. "Of course you aren't. If I felt like this about one of my pupils, I'd be fired."

For about three seconds, my mind went blank. Then I thought, *What what what? What did you say just now? If you felt like this? Like what?*

Nao kept on talking. "Until now, I was never interested in guys who liked me, but for once, it's nice."

Um, what? I don't understand. Translation, please! I needed Doraemon, the cartoon robot-cat, to show up with some Translation Jelly from the next century.

"You mean you have no interest in guys who fall in love with you?"

"Right. Most men like women who like them, but most women are different, I think. We wonder, *Why is this guy into me? If I'm the best he can do, he must not amount to much.* That's how our minds work."

"Then your self-esteem is way too low!"

"Maybe. Anyway, the way you look at me, little hearts coming out of your eyes . . . I don't know, it's actually starting to grow on me a little."

I didn't think I was doing anything so cartoonish, but if it was growing on her, that was fine with me.

"So—you and I are together now."

"Don't get carried away. I said you're getting to me a *little*." She took a step back, beyond the reach of my outstretched arms. "Tell you what. I'll let you have another date."

Then what's changed? Nothing! I sighed. I'd just have to be patient.

Her fingers touched my cheek. Wonderingly, I lifted my face, just as she stood on tiptoe and kissed me. Her lips, dry and soft, pulled away after an instant.

"Bye now. Be careful on the way back."

She turned and went back in the house. I saw her off and then pumped my fist. *Yes!*

No one saw us kiss, and somehow I managed to get home in one piece, even though I was on cloud nine. It was a miracle, all of it.

I wonder if there's a god of love and relationships in Kamusari. If there is, I might make a hundred pilgrimages there.

When the workweek began, I joined my team on the mountain as always, and during lunch I told them about Nao. Not about the kiss, of course. If I didn't keep that a secret, they'd tease me to death.

Which reminds me—I'll have to make sure Granny Shige doesn't read this. She doesn't know how to use the computer, so I'm not worried about her getting into it when I'm away, but when she sees me writing she pesters me, begging to read it. I should probably just tell her I've quit writing.

Anyway, I told my coworkers about Nao finding the pen right after our visit to the shrine. "So Inari really does work wonders," I said.

"Nah," Yoki said. "It was just a coincidence."

"No, it wasn't. Don't forget, Mr. Yamane got his devil stinger back right away after he visited the shrine, too."

They all looked at each other and grinned. What was going on? I didn't like it one bit.

"You're a good kid, Yuki." Old Man Saburo sounded like he might give me a pat on the head or pinch my cheek. Again, I was being treated like a child.

"I'm a normal guy," I said. "Yoki, what are you laughing at?"

Yoki went on chuckling, but he said, "I'm not laughing. I'm being normal." He looked away and poured water from his canteen into the little dish he'd made for Noko out of leaves.

Iwao spoke up grudgingly. "You see, here's the thing. It wasn't the god who delivered the devil stinger to Yamane's house. It was whoever took it in the first place."

"What!" I let out a yell loud enough to knock down some cedar leaves.

"I'll bet as a kid you believed in Santa Claus, too." Yoki grinned and went to put fresh tea leaves in the pot.

"Who took it?"

"Somebody in the village," Old Man Saburo said calmly, "that's for sure. Nobody knows who, but that's all right. The devil stinger's back, so there's no point in tracking down the thief and meting out a punishment."

What a lame ending! Was it really okay to let it go? I was shocked.

Seiichi smiled. "In the village, we place the highest value on relationships. Because relationships are never easy. As far as the devil stinger goes, it's probably best not to aggravate the situation."

"Then O-Inari-san had no part in it after all." After the awe I'd felt, I was deeply let down.

"No, Yuki, you've got it wrong," said Iwao. "Why do you think the thief sneaked the devil stinger back?"

"Guilty conscience?"

"In part. But what made them realize they'd done something wrong? It was hearing that you and Yamane paid that visit to the shrine."

"How so?"

Yoki said proudly, "Anyone born and bred in Kamusari has heard all about Inari and what he's capable of, from the time they were little. They know he dishes out punishments to liars and thieves."

"You mean the thief returned the devil stinger out of fear of what the god might do to him?"

"That's right." Iwao nodded. "When nobody believes in the gods anymore, they lose their power. O-Inari-san is still going strong. He has overwhelming power."

Maybe, but I still felt disillusioned. Inari's miraculous power to restore lost objects boiled down to fear of punishment and pangs of conscience. And yet, I had to concede that his power was truly over-whelming, in a sense. When someone believes in him, Inari lodges in that person's heart. A god who hates lies and loves purity. So from then on, that person is incapable of wrongdoing. Inari keeps constant watch, and his punishments are fearful. Sometimes temptation gets the better of a person and they cheat or otherwise err, but the god in their heart raises a storm of protest, urging them to mend their ways.

Maybe that's what a god is truly like. Someone who's not far off in the sky but right in our hearts, always watching. Keeping an eye on our words and deeds, our lies and our truth.

I think I'll visit the Inari shrine again. Something about it really appeals to me. The fox statues are cute, too. Maybe I'll look around in the forest for wood to make a new torii.

And that ends my lost-and-found tale.

Sigh. What's going to happen in my is-it-or-isn't-it romance with Nao? We did kiss (I'll never tire of remembering!) but now what? Can I be more aggressive? I agonize. I'm afraid of losing my way.

Everybody, please root for me, that I may be lucky in love.

Perhaps if I pay another visit to the shrine, next time I'll have good news to report!

6

THE SIXTH NIGHT

CHRISTMAS IN KAMUSARI

Whew, that was a close call. I almost let the year end without coming up with any topic of interest.

As I wrote last time, Nao and I k-k-k-k-kissed. Actually, I didn't kiss her so much as she kissed me, but anyway, our lips touched. No, joined. Merged!

Sorry. That's not true. It wasn't on the level of joining or merging. It was an extremely chaste and proper *mwah*. But oh, what a shining moment! Wow. Wow. I actually thought, *Maybe I'll get pregnant.* Wow. For a mere kiss to spark thoughts of pregnancy in me, a guy—what imagination, what love!

Sorry. I'm so hyper this must be gross to read. I'm lovesick. But there's just no quieting the pounding of my heart! And it's not only my heart; my cock is constantly on the point of becoming the "unfettered shogun," but gets admonished by Jack—*Sire, restrain yourself!* I feign nonchalance, whiling away my time tossing food to the carp in the lake. In short, I spend my time jacking off. The way I am now, everything I see and hear connects straight to you-know-where. I'm like a kid in junior high. That's me, Yuki Hirano, age twenty. And incidentally, there's no lake in Yoki's front yard. It's just an analogy.

Remembering my k-k-k-k-kiss with Nao set my heart hammering and made me want to run around the mountains, shouting madly, *Nao, I'm ready to join, to merge with you!* I could have gone around gathering pretty feathers, stuck them in my hair for a furious mating dance.

But I didn't. I couldn't even see her. From the middle of December, she was so busy writing report cards and attending meetings, she had no time for anything else. I tried dropping by her house after work more than once, but she was never there. The teachers all worked overtime, it seemed; even well after dark, the teachers' room at Kamusari Elementary was lit up.

That guy who once gave her a lift home in his car was probably in there with her. The thought made me grind my molars almost into my gums. I managed to contain the flames of jealousy, because nobody loves a jealous man. But I found out all I needed to know about who he was. Everybody in Kamusari knows everybody else, so you can learn stuff just by asking around. I asked Miho. She and Yoki have no children and so no direct connection with the school, but she was a fount of information:

"The young male teacher at Kamusari Elementary? Oh, you mean Mr. Okuda. He's from Nagoya originally, but he came to Mie for college, I heard. He lives alone in Hisai. Commutes to work by car."

He doesn't know me, but now I know his name. That puts me ahead! He doesn't even know I'm his rival. Look out, Okuda! You'll never beat me! If you think you're going to get a date with Nao for Christmas, you've got another thing coming!

That's right. I had a secret longing to spend Christmas with Nao— starting Christmas Eve, if possible. Santa had told me that this year, the closing ceremony for the second term would be held on December 25. Surely she wasn't planning to sit up all night the night before, finishing up report cards. Surely she'd have time to spare on Christmas Eve.

But where in Kamusari could we go for a romantic Christmas date? What if Okuda sneaked ahead of me and invited her on a drive to Nagoya or Tsu? I was determined to get a commitment from her before he did. But December 24 was a regular workday for me, so even if I was able to borrow Yoki's pickup, we couldn't go anyplace far. Still, I really wanted to be with her on Christmas Eve. I was always going to phone her, but I kept putting it off. Even though we'd kissed once, if she turned down a Christmas date with me, I might never recover. There was a big chance she'd brush me off: *Sorry. Busy.* For someone so passionate, she acts cold to guys who like her, just to give them a hard time. Of course, I find even that quirk endearing (tolerance being the mark of a mature adult, ahem).

Obsessed with the fear of being turned down, I couldn't bring myself to ask her out. Meanwhile, I worked like a demon. We were super-busy cutting and harvesting timber on all the mountains around Kamusari before it started to snow. Because of the danger involved, all of us were tense, and the felled timber weighed a ton, even though we let it dry out a bit on the slopes before hauling it out. We use heavy equipment, but it takes muscle power, too. After work, I'd be so worn out that I couldn't think of anything but supper and bed. One time I fell asleep at the table. Yoki teased me: "All of a sudden you conked out—I thought you were dead!" Even when my cheek landed on the table, I didn't wake up, apparently. Yoki carried me to my room.

Yoki and Miho knew I was taking Nao on drives, so they were curious about how our relationship was coming along. One night Granny Shige came into my room and whispered, "You and she kissed, eh?" I was just falling asleep, but that woke me right up—I nearly jumped out of my skin.

"How did you know?"

She knelt on the tatami and smiled complacently. "ESP." Turning toward the computer in the corner, she raised her hands like a magician. "When I do this, I can read everything in there, clear as day."

"Liar. It's not plugged in."

"The older, the wiser. The older, the wiser." Muttering this like a spell, she tottered to her feet and left the room.

Weird.

It was hard to believe she knew how to use the computer. Maybe she'd tricked me into an admission. The file was on the computer desktop. Maybe I should hide it deeper inside the computer. I wrestled with what to do, but in the end I was too sleepy to do anything.

In between felling trees and hauling timber, I found some wood to use for a new torii for the Inari shrine. I looked through logs left over from forest thinning that had no sales value and picked a few that were solid and well dried. Iwao helped me load them onto his truck. One way or another, I managed to fashion a new torii. It was small, just high enough for an adult to pass through, and the crossbeam was nailed in place, though that's not the traditional way. When it was done, Iwao gave it a coat of varnish, so even though it wasn't painted red, it looked good. I was glad. O-Inari-san would be pleased, I thought. I intended it as thanks for the return of Nao's fountain pen.

We called on muscleman Yoki for help, and the three of us lugged the new torii up to the shrine and replaced the old one. While I was there, I went and stood before the shrine. But Inari is the god of finding lost or stolen objects, so I wasn't sure how to proceed. *She stole something I can't live without—my heart!* Was that what I ought to say? But what if Inari then punished her? That would be terrible.

Turning it over in my mind, I stood with my palms pressed together. Yoki gave me a sidelong glance and grinned. "If you're asking O-Inari-san for something, you've gotta say it out loud."

Iwao nodded. "Yep, that's how it's done."

All right, then. If that's the way they wanted it, fine. I said in a loud voice, "Please let me have a Christmas date with Nao!"

Inari must have been stunned, getting asked to do something so far outside his specialty.

Making a new torii wasn't all I did.

One Sunday evening, Santa came over. The door was unlocked, as usual. When I heard him call my name by the front door, I invited him in, but instead of taking off his shoes and stepping up to join us around the *kotatsu* heater, he stood there in the earthen entryway, fidgeting.

"What's up? Don't just stand there in the cold. Come on up and get warm."

"No, that's okay."

He didn't seem his usual self. Yoki, Miho, and Grandma Shige had been watching TV, but now all eyes were on Santa. He hung his head, then raised his eyes and looked at me.

"Um, Yu-chan?"

"Yeah?"

"Have you heard of Christmas?"

"Well, uh . . ."

I thought fast. Santa had never heard of Christmas! I was surprised, yet I could understand. Kamusari district was the remotest part of the village, and he was the only school-age kid around. He was surrounded by old men and women, and his father, as the master, had to respect village traditions, not imported Western ones. He must've found out about Christmas for the first time after becoming a first grader.

How to answer? If I said, *Yeah, I know all about it,* then Santa might feel bad to think he was the only one who didn't know. Also, for all I knew, Seiichi had kept him in the dark for a reason. Maybe he had deliberately avoided Christmas.

But before I could say anything, Yoki burst out, "You're kidding! Santa, you never heard of Christmas?" Nobody is better at wrecking someone's attempt to be tactful. At his thoughtless remark, Santa looked ready to cry.

"I've *heard* of it," I said cautiously, "but you know, Christmas is really nothing to shout about." My words stabbed me in the heart. If I couldn't get a date with Nao, then this year's Christmas would truly be nothing to shout about.

Seeing Santa on the point of tears seemed to make Yoki think better of what he had said. "Yeah," he said. "It's just an old man with a beard and the same name as you, sneaking in people's houses in the middle of the night, that's all."

He made Santa Claus sound like a thief or a monster!

Miho had heard enough. "Santa, have a tangerine." She went over and handed him a piece of fruit.

"Thank you." He sat on the edge of the raised floor, legs dangling, and ate the tangerine.

When she saw that he had recovered his composure, Miho said, "Now what's this all about? What do you think Christmas is, Santa?"

"Dai-chan and Mihiro-chan"—two friends of his, apparently—"said that at Christmas everybody decorates a tree, like we do bamboo at the star festival."

"Well, not exactly like that," I said. "At the star festival you write out your wish on a piece of colored paper and hang it up. Christmas tree decorations are more like stars and glittery balls, I think."

"Thank you for the tangerine. It was good." Santa folded the peel neatly and handed it to me. What manners! Then he said, "Oh, and they said if you eat fried chicken before you go to bed, then while you're sleeping Santa comes and puts something nice in your socks. I never wear socks to bed. You think that's why Santa's never come to my house?"

I didn't know what to say. His description of Christmas customs made the holiday sound weird.

"Anyway," Santa wound up, "they say it's really fun. So I want to have Christmas, too!"

The rest of us exchanged looks. Yoki's eyes said, *You handle this.*

I had no choice but to ask the question we all had in mind: "Did you ask your daddy about Christmas?"

"Yeah."

"What'd he say?"

"He said he'd think about it. What is there to think about?"

"Maybe he's trying to decide if he should leave the front door unlocked so Santa can come in."

"Our front door's always unlocked."

"Then he's trying to decide how much chicken meat to buy for the fried chicken."

"I dunno." Santa seemed unconvinced. It wouldn't do to give him a hint that his father would be Santa Claus.

"It's getting dark," I said, dodging the issue. "Come on, I'll walk you home."

We left, and for some reason Yoki came along.

I can never get over how big Seiichi's place is. It has a huge name-plate in front, reading "Nakamura Lumber Co."

Santa opened the door and went in. The earthen entryway connects straight to the kitchen, where his mother stood making supper. The delicious smell of miso filled the air.

"You're back! Santa, where were you? Did you do your homework?"

"Not yet!" he said clearly. He turned and waved to Yoki and me before going on into the house.

"Well, hurry up and get it done." Risa was stirring something with a ladle. She turned, saw us standing there, and smiled. "Oh! Hi there," she started to say, but Yoki cut her off, gesturing and mouthing the words *Is Seiichi here?*

She nodded and called, "Dear, could you come here a minute?"

Seiichi poked his head out, and when he saw us, he slipped his feet into a pair of straw sandals and stepped down to join us. "What is it? Did something happen?"

"C'mere." Yoki grabbed him by the arm and pulled him outside. "Santa found out about Santa."

For a moment, Seiichi looked bewildered. Then he nodded. "Yeah, lately he's been pestering me about wanting to celebrate Christmas."

"Why shouldn't he?"

"Is it because you're the master, and it's not cool for you to celebrate a foreign holiday?" I asked.

Seiichi laughed. "No, nothing like that. The trouble is, he wants a special robot toy. Something to do with a kids' show he watches Sunday mornings."

"Go ahead and buy it for him," said Yoki grandly.

"It costs five thousand yen."

"That's a lot."

"One of these days, Santa will run Nakamura Lumber." Seiichi folded his arms. "It would be unfortunate for the mountains, and the people who work on them, if the next master were someone accustomed to luxury. That's why I'm trying to figure out how best to handle Christmas."

So in parenting Santa, Seiichi had the future of the village in mind. This surprised me. On the other hand, I could see that forestry wouldn't be a good fit for someone who was interested in cool clothes, kick-ass cars, and avoiding danger and insects. When I first came to the village, I used to think, *It's always too hot or too cold. The work's too hard. Life here sucks.*

But gradually I was drawn to the beauty and power of the mountains. The rustle of leaves as the wind sweeps the mountainside; the damp, sweet smell of soil; the shifting cloud shadows; the sense of animals in bushes nearby, watching and holding their breath. All that became part of me, and I began to enjoy life here. A pickup truck is the handiest way to get around, and as for clothes, nobody sees what you're wearing but birds and monkeys. I've come to think that as long as Nao doesn't mind, I can wear any old thing. If I can eat and sleep and go work in the mountains, what more do I need?

Maybe I was never suited to city life in the first place. When I lived in Yokohama, I was pretty much always bored.

Yeah, five thousand yen for a kid's toy is expensive, but Christmas comes only once a year. It seemed okay to me. Santa was a good kid, way smarter than me, and I couldn't see him turning into a spoiled brat just because he got a Christmas present when he was seven. But Seiichi wanted to teach him values like patience and respect, because one day he would bear the weight of the mountains of Kamusari. He was a prince who had to learn to be king (or as Yoki said, "king of the mountain").

"Why not find a way to celebrate Christmas without spending money?" I suggested hesitantly. "Santa seems just as excited about decorating a tree and eating something special as he is about presents. All you would need is some fried chicken, and you could easily cut down a Christmas tree. Why don't we have a party and enjoy Christmas together?"

"Great idea!" Yoki clapped his hands. "Don't worry about a present, Seiichi. Just get him something else."

"Maybe so." Then Seiichi turned to me with a quizzical smile. "But Yuki, are you sure that would be all right with you?"

"Of course. Why wouldn't it be?"

"Well, if there's a party, then . . ."

"That's right!" Yoki exclaimed. "Then you couldn't ask Nao on a date."

Oh, no! I'd been so focused on making Santa have a good time, I forgot all about my plan for a special Christmas date with Nao. How could I?

Wait. Nao lived alone, and she was Risa's little sister. If she heard Seiichi was hosting a Christmas party, she'd be sure to come. That would make it a lot easier to invite her, and I'd be able to spend Christmas with her, which was my original goal anyway.

Oh, but dammit. Nao was gone on Seiichi. Seeing him be a devoted husband and father would surely be painful for her, and looking on, knowing how she felt, would be painful for me. I was torn. What to do? Still, a party was way better than her going on a date with Okuda—or, heaven forbid, spending Christmas Eve and Christmas all alone.

"I don't mind at all," I said, forcing a smile. "I wasn't especially thinking of asking Nao out, anyway."

"Oh, really!" Yoki hooted like an owl and grinned.

And so, thanks to my suggestion, Seiichi decided to throw a Christmas party. Besides me, the guest list included Old Man Saburo, Iwao and his wife, Yoki and his family, and Nao.

I phoned Nao. I expected her to be out, but she picked up right away, maybe because it was Sunday night. Even with the news of the party to share, talking to her on the phone made me nervous, as always.

"Santa doesn't know it yet, but on the night of the twenty-fourth, there's going to be a Christmas party at his place, and you're invited. Will you come?"

After a moment of silence, she said, "Yes. What do I need to do? Will we exchange presents?"

"No, nothing like that. We'll pick out a tree and cut it down, and Miho, Risa, and Iwao's wife are going to do the cooking."

"I hate to make them do all the work."

"You're busy with school. Don't worry about it. They said to come on over as soon as school lets out, and not to bring a thing."

"I appreciate that. But tell them I'll bring a salad."

"Okay, I will."

"Say, Yuki?"

"What?"

"Never mind."

"Good night."

"G'night."

What had she started to say? It bothered me, but the next day was Monday, and I had to work in the mountains. I took a quick bath and crawled in the futon.

So—Christmas with Nao! (And Yoki and company, but that was okay.) I was as excited as Santa. I couldn't stop smiling. I thought about what kind of present I should get for her. What would she like?

Out in the yard, Noko started howling. Maybe there was a full moon. The cold was bitter that night.

We set out to look for a Christmas tree.

"It's supposed to be a fir tree, right?" Old Man Saburo asked.

This stumped me. The mountains of Kamusari are almost all planted with trees. Here and there, zelkova or camphor trees grow naturally, but for whatever reason—maybe the climate is too warm?—I've never seen a fir tree around Kamusari.

"With all these trees, you'd think there'd be one fir tree somewhere!" Yoki grumbled.

We were standing at the foot of East Mountain, looking up. The neatly aligned trees were all cedars and cypresses.

"This one will do, won't it?" Seiichi rapped his knuckles on a red pine. It had taken root and grown naturally by the side of the road, managing to thrive despite heavy competition from surrounding cedars and cypresses. The trunk was five inches around, the height a good six feet. The tree was still young.

Yoki scoffed. "Seiichi, sometimes you're really sketchy, you know that? A pine tree and a fir tree are completely different! A cypress'd be more like it."

"Maybe so," said Iwao, "but this pine has a nice shape to it." He inspected the tree closely, more than I thought necessary. It wasn't as if we were going to transplant it in Seiichi's yard.

"And it's got red bark and green leaves," said Old Man Saburo. "Christmas colors." He was really going out of his way to put a positive spin on it.

In the end, the decision was Seiichi's. "It's right by the road, so it'll be easy to carry out. This is the one."

His word was absolute. Reluctantly, Yoki got into position with his ax. After tapping the trunk of the red pine twice with the handle, he swung. *Thwack. Thwack.* The sounds resonated out across the mountains. Noko wagged his tail as if keeping time.

In no time, the pine fell. Noko ran up, raised a leg in the air, and peed on it. He seemed to understand that this one wasn't for sale.

"Cut it out, Noko. This one's for Christmas." I picked him up. The confused look on his face said, *Christmas? Come again?*

We loaded the pine tree in Seiichi's pickup. Later, we'd put it somewhere inconspicuous in his yard. Then we started up the mountainside on foot, on our way to the day's work site. We were going to thin a stand of cypress near the peak of East Mountain. We soon spread out and set to work. The chain saw rang out, along with the sound of Yoki's ax.

After stopping for lunch, we worked again in the afternoon. Around two o'clock, something like ash skimmed the tip of my nose. I looked up at the sky.

"It's snowing!"

The first snow of this winter came floating down; the flakes slipped between cypress leaves and softly covered the ground.

Soon Seiichi came to find me. "Yuki, let's call it a day."

I gathered up my things, shouldered the chain saw, and followed after him. When the team was assembled, we went single file down the slope, heading for the road. Noko seemed excited by the snow, leaping and bounding along.

"The first snow came early this year," said Yoki.

"We might be in for a cold spell," said Old Man Saburo.

"Whatever happened to global warming?" wondered Iwao.

They chattered away as usual, but I couldn't join in. The new snow made the slope slippery and treacherous. I had to pick my way carefully, eyes on the ground. Conversation was beyond me.

Seiichi was quiet, too, working something over in his mind. "I'm thinking of not doing snow removal this winter," he said. He was referring to the process of tying ropes to cedars and cypresses bent over by the weight of the snow and pulling them straight, freeing them from the weight of the snow. If that isn't done, their trunks will grow bent and twisted or even break in two.

"What?" said Yoki. "Why not?"

"Lately everybody's shorthanded, so a lot of places have stopped doing it. And there's a theory that once a tree bends under snow, it never will grow properly, even if it's straightened out."

"Then what'd we knock ourselves out for, all this time?" Yoki sounded shocked.

Old Man Saburo offered comfort. "Forestry techniques get refined. If better ways of doing things come along, we need to accept them."

"True," said Iwao, "but it seems kind of drastic to do it all at once. Seiichi, how about this? Decide which slopes we'll leave alone and which we won't, and keep careful records. Do that for several years, and if the trees don't show any difference in the way they grow, then just leave them all be."

"You're right. Let's do that." Seiichi nodded.

The master may be an absolute figure, but he's no tyrant. He takes into account tradition and the feelings of the men who work on the mountains, and he's willing to talk things over. That's why we all trust Seiichi.

Yoki held out his palm to catch snowflakes. "At this rate, we might not be able to work tomorrow."

"In that case," said Old Man Saburo, "I'd like to go visit my son and his family."

That got my attention. "You have a son?"

"Yep. He lives in Nagoya." Old Man Saburo, a widower, lived alone in the village. "I go see him and his family once a year. If I go at New Year's, we can't relax and be ourselves. If they come to the village to see me, I'm all alone, and I can't show them any real hospitality." Also, he said, his younger brother had injured his back and was laid up in a hospital in Nagoya. If he went now, he could see him, too.

"I'll go with you to Nagoya," I said.

"What for?" asked Yoki. "Don't tell me you want to buy new clothes for the party and get all gussied up."

"You know me better than that. Anyway, it's only going to be us at the party, so why dress up? I want to buy some presents."

"For Nao."

"For Santa!" Well, for Nao, too. But I wished he wouldn't just come out with it so baldly in front of everyone. The man doesn't have a shred of tact.

"All right," said Seiichi. "If the snow piles up tonight, we'll take tomorrow off."

Thanks to the snow, we got home early. Yoki and I took turns soaking in the tub, and then relaxed in the family room till supper. Granny Shige was sitting at the kotatsu heater, cutting construction paper with scissors and spreading out origami paper from an empty cookie box.

"What are you doing?" I asked.

"Making decorations."

"Oh, for the Christmas tree!"

"Yep."

"I'll help."

I borrowed scissors and paste and cut out a star shape, then decorated it with origami paper. It was kind of lopsided, and the origami paper gave it a distinctly Japanese flavor, but it was okay. Granny Shige made origami cranes and whatnot, and attached strings to hang them from the branches. This was going to be a Japanese-flavored Christmas tree all the way.

"I'll do some, too," Yoki said. He folded a piece of origami paper and cut slits in it, so that when you spread it out, it was like a reed screen. Nice, but that was a decoration for the summertime star festival, not Christmas.

Making things was a lot of fun. After supper, Miho tried her hand, too. "Aren't there Christmas decorations that look like a doll?" she said, and started rolling tissue into a ball. When she was finished, she had made a *teru teru bozu*—the little doll that kids hang up the night before a school outing so it won't rain. I didn't comment.

We put all the decorations in a cardboard box. We planned to decorate the tree on the night of the twenty-third. It was fun to imagine how excited Santa would be when he saw the tree the next morning. Even if it was a red pine and not a fir tree.

The next day, a fine, cold rain was falling. There were two or three inches of snow on the ground, but it was bound to melt and turn to slush. The footing would be bad, so we had the day off, after all.

Old Man Saburo came to pick me up at 9:00 a.m. He was wearing a jacket, for once. I was dressed in my old Yokohama street clothes, too. Neither of us was used to seeing the other in anything but work clothes, so we both laughed.

"There's snow on the road. Will it be safe to drive?" I asked.

"Oh, sure. Around here, in December everybody switches to snow tires."

I had never noticed. Then I remembered Yoki driving his pickup to Matsuyama Motors one day without saying why.

I got in Old Man Saburo's truck, and we were off. The snow on the ground was like sherbet. The tires made squishy, scrunchy noises as we carefully descended the steep mountain road.

"I wonder if we'll make the train," he said.

There's one local train every hour in the village, and that's it. The railroad was supposed to link Matsusaka and Nabari, but unfortunately the tracks end in the middle of the mountains. The closest station is the end of the line. It's not all that close, either; from the village to the station is about an hour by car.

"It'll be tight," I said. "And if it snows again before evening, the trains might stop running."

"You're right. I'll drive all the way to Tsu."

He made a sharp turn and chose the road to Tsu. Once the ground leveled out, there was hardly any snow left. He drove along at a good clip. I looked out the window at the mountains, which were dyed white.

"Why did your brother leave the village?" I asked.

"He's a lot younger than me," said Old Man Saburo, not taking his eyes from the road. "By the time he was grown up and deciding on his path, forestry was in decline. I thought he'd have a better future if he got a company job in the city. He always said heavy labor wasn't for him, anyway."

Forestry was hard work, it was true, but there was also a lot to like about it, I thought.

When I didn't comment, Old Man Saburo said soothingly, "Things are different now. With more young folks like you coming to work in the mountains, times are better. Looking back, I think when my brother was young, society and I were both convinced the best thing you could do was work like a demon and make a pile of money."

"I'd never fit in to that kind of society."

"I didn't see it at the time, but that kind of thinking was a strait-jacket." He shook his head. "But thanks to eager young folks like yourself, the business has changed. I've been in forestry during its heyday and its decline, and the way it is now is the best. Gives me hope that forestry can adapt and grow in the coming years."

I hoped so, too. I hoped that a hundred years from now, the mountains of Kamusari would be unchanged, alongside the villagers. Unique festivals; Oyamazumi-san, O-Inari-san, and Nagahiko the snake god. A village where traditions were cherished and residents tended the forest, planting trees and cutting them down, all while falling in love and quarreling, living out their lives. That was the future I wanted for Kamusari.

A hundred years! The future seemed so far off, like a dream that vanishes when you wake up. But someday, maybe Santa's son would fell a tree I had planted. Thinking of it that way, the future seemed close and familiar. Strange.

I have to do my best, I thought. A quirk of fate had brought me to the village, but now that I lived there, I needed to master forestry, give it everything I had. Besides, if I failed, I wouldn't be able to face Nao.

Old Man Saburo pulled into the parking lot across the street from Tsu Station, and we got on the Kintetsu line. It was an hour's ride to Nagoya on the Limited Express. We sat across from each other in box seats.

"Have you ever celebrated Christmas before?" I asked.

"Of course I have. I'm not that old."

I was surprised to think that Christmas had penetrated into such a remote corner of Japan that far back. "What did you do?"

"I've got two children, the boy in Nagoya and a married daughter in Tokyo. When they were little, they wanted Christmas, just like Santa does. Their mother made curry."

"Doesn't sound all that Christmassy."

"Kids like curry. And they got presents, too."

"Don't tell me you dressed up as Santa."

"Nope, I wore a lion's mask."

"What! How come?"

"Now that the village is shrinking, the lion dance has fallen by the wayside, but back then it was big. It happened to be my turn to wear the lion's head."

That was hardly a reason.

He'd been practicing the dance and had the lion's head at home, he said, so he put it on and sneaked into the children's room while they were sleeping. "I laid their presents by their pillows. My daughter saw me, let out a scream, and started to cry. That woke her brother up, and he wet the bed and started blubbering, too. Their mother got mad and said I was an idiot. Oh, I had quite a time, I'll tell you."

It sounded pretty traumatic for his kids. I could see that even years ago, Christmas in Kamusari hadn't retained much of its original form.

We split up at Nagoya Station and agreed to meet up again at four o'clock. I was free till then. Being in the city again after so long kind of hurt my eyes as I took it all in: shiny new commodities, sparkly women. I felt like a monk just returning to civilization after undergoing austerities in the mountains.

I didn't know my way around Nagoya. I went into the huge department store across from the Japan Railway Station. The upper floors seemed to be a hotel. Anyway, it was gorgeous.

The crowd of shoppers was incredible. I looked at the counters in a trance. I didn't have all that much money to spend. What should I get her?

Then my eye fell on a red scarf. It was a nice deep red, not too flashy. I reached out stealthily to feel it, and it was soft and warm. For a biker, what could be better? The color would go well with her green Kawasaki, too, I thought.

I checked the price tag. More than I'd expected, but not beyond my reach. I walked around to make sure nothing else appealed to me more, and then I bought it and had it gift wrapped. The clerk used paper with a design of tiny Santas and fir trees and finished it off with a red bow.

Right after that, I spotted a pair of child-sized blue gloves. Perfect for Santa. Next to them were some pink ones for an adult. The two pairs were a set, with yellow and brown stars on the back. I remembered that Granny Shige wore work gloves to keep her hands warm. Pink seemed a bit on the cute side for her, but I decided to get them anyway.

I bought both pairs of gloves and had them wrapped, too. Now, what to get Yoki and Miho?

For the first time, I realized how much fun it is to look for presents. When I was in high school, I used to go shopping with my then girlfriend, and I picked out a Christmas present for her, too. But it felt, I don't know, like something I *had* to do. Like, *she's sure to get me something, so it's a pain, but I gotta get her something.* That wasn't very nice of me. For all I know, she may have spent a lot of time picking out something she thought I'd like.

I got on the escalator and looked at all the different sales counters. There was a nice set of indigo his-and-hers rice bowls, the bigger one for the man and the smaller one for the wife, so I got those for Yoki and Miho. If it was a present, maybe she'd think twice before throwing it at him.

By then it was after one o'clock. I'd spent two hours shopping, so no wonder I was hungry. I left the department store and went into the underground shopping mall, picked a place at random, and ordered the *misokatsu* lunch—a deep-fried pork cutlet with miso-flavored sauce and all the trimmings. I'd never had misokatsu before; it tasted great. The salty-sweet flavor could get to be a habit, I thought.

After lunch, there was plenty of time till four o'clock. Carrying my bagful of presents, I went outside. A thick layer of clouds still covered the sky, but it had stopped raining. I walked down a street with no particular destination in mind. It was so wide it made me nervous. I went into a coffee shop and read a manga magazine while drinking orange juice. (For some reason, along with the juice they served me a cup of tea made of powdered kelp and pickled plum. Maybe it was the shop's specialty?)

In Kamusari, if I walked along the street, people would call out to me. Here in Nagoya, nobody paid me any attention; the thought was really refreshing, and at the same time kind of sad. It's strange, the way wherever you are, you feel like there's too much of some things and not enough of others. I wonder if it's that way for everybody.

After killing some more time, I met up with Old Man Saburo as planned, and we went back to Kamusari. He'd had lunch with his son and daughter-in-law, and, though the timing was tight, he had squeezed in a visit to his brother, too. He found to his relief that his brother was due to be released from the hospital in a couple of days.

"*You take care of your back, too,* he tells me, the smart aleck. Ha! I'll have you know I can still make it down the mountain carrying two cedars across my shoulders!"

Old Man Saburo, you're pushing eighty, I wanted to tell him. *You don't have to be that strong anymore.*

On the night of the twenty-third, Yoki and I went over to Seiichi's place. Yoki was carrying the cardboard box with all the decorations inside, so he held the flashlight in his mouth. (I always knew he had a big mouth.) I told him he didn't have to do that, since I had a flashlight, too, but he insisted: "I'll light my own way, thank you." But because he had the flashlight in his mouth, it came out more like *I yi yi ohn ay, ank yu.* He's crazy.

There was a big hole in the yard where we would plant the tree. Seiichi, Iwao, and Old Man Saburo had dug it together.

"Santa's asleep. Try not to make any noise," said Seiichi.

We nodded silently and then together carried the red pine over from a corner of the yard and stuck it in the hole. It was hard getting it to stand up straight. Yoki braced it with his back. "That's it, hold it there," Iwao said in a low voice and started to fill in the hole. I helped.

What were we doing, digging in the yard in the middle of the night? It felt as if we were a gang of robbers, burying stolen gold.

Seiichi and Old Man Saburo stomped on the soil around the pine tree to firm it. The tree stood erect, a little taller than any of us.

"Okay, let's start decorating!" Yoki brought out a stepladder, beer cases, and other things to stand on. We all started hanging decorations wherever we wanted.

Old Man Saburo looked worriedly at the origami stars. "Might need something brighter."

Iwao pulled out a set of colorful Christmas lights. "I found these in my shed."

"Perfect," said Yoki, stringing the lights on the tree. "Seiichi, go get an extension cord."

When the lights were strung, Seiichi plugged the extension cord into a socket in the shed and turned on the switch.

Cries of admiration went up.

The red pine looked like a space alien whose head bulged in back.

"It looks funny after all, because it's not a fir tree," said Yoki.

"But it's festive," I said. "And Christmassy."

"It'll do just fine," said Iwao.

The next morning, we gathered as usual in Seiichi's yard and warmed ourselves at the fire in the oilcan while we talked about the day's work—but we couldn't take our eyes off the tree decked out in the middle of the yard. None of us could wait to see Santa's face when he came out.

Finally the door opened and out flew Santa, his school satchel on his back. "Bye!" The next moment, he saw the red pine in the yard. "A Christmas tree! Daddy, did you make it?"

"We all made it together," Seiichi said calmly.

"Thank you, thank you, thank you!" Santa was wreathed in smiles. "Wow, it's great! A real Christmas tree!"

He ran around and around the tree, looking up at its branches as if he couldn't believe his eyes. Noko ran with him, pausing again to mark his territory.

"Noko! No!" Santa gently pushed the dog away, laughing. Seeing how thrilled he was, I felt all the sorrier we didn't get him a genuine fir tree.

"If you don't hurry, you'll miss the bus," said Risa. "Come straight home after school, okay?"

Santa had no way of knowing it, but today was the big day—the day of the Christmas party.

"Okay! See ya!" He finally stopped circling the tree and left.

"If we had the party and Santa Claus showed up, that kid'd be so tickled he'd wet his pants," said Yoki.

"The lion's head is just over in the assembly hall. Want me to go get it?" Old Man Saburo said teasingly to me.

I vetoed the idea for Santa's sake. "Don't, or he really might wet his pants!"

Whew. I'm only typing at the keyboard, but my hands and my brain are tired. I'll stop here for now. I'll report on the Christmas party next time. Some of you may be wondering how Nao and I got on, what the atmosphere was like. Well, actually, it was a party like a million others.

Readers, are you dressed warmly against the cold, like me? Or are you heading into summer? Either way, don't catch cold!

I've gotten better at pretending I have readers. Oh, that reminds me—to keep Granny Shige from reading this, I'll have to bury it somewhere in the depths of the computer.

Till next time!

7

THE FINAL NIGHT

EASY LIVING IN KAMUSARI

On Christmas Eve, after finishing my fried chicken, I said to Nao, "Come with me to the storehouse for a minute, will you?"

"Okay, but why?"

"You know why. So we can be alone, of course."

"Oh, Yuki. What a love-rascal you are!"

Nao blushed, but she slipped out of Seiichi's house with me. It had been snowing all evening and the ground was covered in a thick layer of white. The mountainsides, too, were white against the night sky. The party guests had left footprints when they arrived, and these were starting to disappear in the falling snow. Nao and I walked away from them, toward the storehouse.

The moment I opened the storehouse door and smelled the slightly musty smell of the interior, I said, "Nao, I can't wait anymore."

"No, Yuki, you mustn't. This is too sudden."

"No, it isn't."

"You're crazy. You really are a love-rascal."

Despite her words, she was smiling as I held her tight. Encouraged, I shoved her down and . . .

Hey, hey, Granny Shige! How'd you get in here? I had the computer locked, with a password, so how the heck did you find my secret file?

Everybody, please don't get the wrong idea. I definitely did not shove Nao down in a storehouse on Christmas Eve. Those opening lines are something Granny Shige dreamed up on her own.

They're kind of interesting, so I'll save them. But really—*So we can be alone, of course. I can't wait anymore.* What kind of person does Granny Shige think I am? Why does it read like a soap opera? (I've hardly ever watched one, but I have an idea what they're like.)

When I saw Granny Shige sitting by herself in front of the computer, I was blown away. The screen cast a bluish light on her face, and for one second, I thought, *It's a monster!* Then I went charging into the room.

"Granny Shige! You can use a computer?"

Caught red-handed, she turned to me with a guilty look. "Yuki, back already?"

"Yes. What's the matter, you didn't want me to come back? What did you do while I was away?"

"Your novel stops in the middle, so I was continuing it for you."

"Who said you could do that?" (And it's not a novel. For the record, it's a record.) "I had it set not to open without a password. How'd you get in?"

"I know the letters of the alphabet as well as anyone." She looked proud. "And your password wasn't hard to figure out. All I did was guess what was on your mind. Easy. I typed in NAO, and bingo."

Crap. All the strength drained out of me. I crumpled to the floor, fists on the tatami. "You can type!"

She smiled, a complacent look on her face. "I watched from the side while you did it, and I joined a computer class at the eldercare center. There are a few things I still can't figure out, though. Maybe you can teach me."

"No. And from now on, hands off that computer!"

"You're a crouch!" *Crouch* is the Kamusari word for someone who won't share. And in Granny Shige's opus (?), the word *love-rascal* that Nao uses means a lecher, someone obsessed with sex.

Granny Shige stood up in a huff, though she moved very deliberately, and announced, "I'll go feed the goldfish," before leaving the room at a pace slower than a turtle's.

Whew. Man, you just can't let down your guard. I had that file hidden away deep inside the computer. But all along, Granny Shige was watching and improving her computer skills on the sly, as if forgetting she's an old lady who looks like a mummified bean-jam bun! I checked to make sure she had closed the door all the way and then immediately changed my password to SHIGE. I was embarrassed she'd guessed my first password so easily.

Of course, I can understand why she'd be anxious to know what happened that night. It's true that I stopped writing this secret record for a while, but that's because I went home to Yokohama for New Year's. Then when I came back after vacation, the first thing I saw was a monster—no, I mean Granny Shige—hunched over the computer. My mind reeled. I tell you, Kamusari is dangerous—you've gotta be more on your toes here than in Yokohama!

Everybody, I bet you're all wondering about the party, too, and what happened between Nao and me. Am I right? You do want to know, don't you? Please say you do. I know you guys don't actually exist, but let me pretend I'm writing this to satisfy you, or I'll be so embarrassed, my face will be on fire.

I'm still not over the shock of finding out Granny Shige read what I wrote (and added to it!), but I intend to pull myself together and write about what happened on Christmas Eve, from beginning to end. Stay with me, everyone!

On the night of December 24, Yoki, Granny Shige, and I set out for Seiichi's house. Yoki carried Granny Shige on his back, and I carried the bag of presents I'd bought in Nagoya. Noko wanted to go to the Christmas party, too, I guess; anyway, he trotted along.

The Seiichi Nakamura team had been at work in the mountains all day, and the wives had been at Seiichi's all afternoon, cooking.

It was completely dark out. The second we stepped out of the house, my ears stung. The wind sweeping down from the mountains was so cold, it hurt. Snow had just started to fall and lightly covered the ground. Granny Shige was wearing a padded, sleeveless coat, and I held a black umbrella over her. Snowflakes landed on the umbrella with a gentle brushing sound.

There were fresh footprints in the snow, of two kinds. Those made by rubber boots walking straight ahead belonged to Iwao, and those made by jikatabi, with various side excursions along the way, belonged to Old Man Saburo. Both sets of footprints led through Seiichi's yard to his front door. There were no motorcycle tire tracks, so Nao hadn't yet arrived. Maybe making salad was taking longer than she expected? I didn't really associate Nao with cooking (if making salad is cooking; I guess it is).

The red pine Christmas tree was all lit up, standing there in the swirling snow like a gaudy space alien. It struck me as pretty and rather sad, or else silly and really peculiar. I was unable to sort out my feelings as we passed by the tree and went up to the house.

Yoki managed to open the front door with his foot. Warm air came rushing out, along with assorted appetizing smells. We scarcely had time to register the delicious warmth before Santa came speeding toward us like a bullet.

"Yu-chan!" He looked up at us, beaming. "Thanks for making a Christmas party!"

"It's gonna be great, Santa." I tousled his hair. "Lots of good eats!"

In the kitchen, Risa, Miho, and Iwao's wife were arranging food on big platters. I saw *chirashizushi* (sushi rice scattered with colorful toppings), *oinari-san,* braised pork belly, and salt-grilled sea bream. There were vegetable dishes, too—spinach with sesame tofu, dried radish strips, fried tofu with vegetables, *hijiki* seaweed—and more, including, of course, fried chicken. It was truly a feast.

Yoki let Noko in the earthen entryway, with Risa's permission. Noko twitched his nose in seeming amazement at all the rich smells, sniffing and sniffing.

In the main room, Seiichi, Iwao, and Old Man Saburo had started drinking beer. They were talking with great animation and gestures, clearly enjoying themselves. The party was well underway, I thought, and then I heard what they were saying.

Iwao: "One went for a fancy price at the lumber fair, I heard."

Seiichi: "Yes, a hundred-twenty-year-old cypress. Solid, no hollows."

Old Man Saburo: "Amazing. Where was it from?"

Seiichi: "The back of East Mountain. The owner is Kawada from Shimo."

Iwao: "How much did it go for?"

Seiichi: "About this much" (holding up several fingers).

Old Man Saburo: "Ooh, that's a pretty price."

Iwao: "Kawada must be tickled pink. We can't let him get all the glory. You know that mountain of yours west of Mt. Kamusari, Seiichi? Aren't a lot of the cedars there well past the century mark?"

Seiichi: "Too soon to cut those down. That'd be a waste. In another twenty years—"

Iwao: "—they'll be close to a hundred fifty years old."

Old Man Saburo: "All right, then, let's hold off some more, let 'em get niiiice and big."

They laughed together like conspirators.

Talking shop at a party! Hard to fathom how much those three loved forestry. And with money involved, their chuckles gave off a whiff of connivance. But fellas, twenty years from now . . . Just how long did Old Man Saburo plan to live? I was impressed that they took the easygoing, long view, Kamusari style, even where profit was concerned. They were patient to a fault.

"Naa-naa," Yoki called out as he came in. (In this case, the word didn't mean "Let's take our time" but "Hey, nice night, isn't it!") "Looks like I'm a little late."

"Oh, Yoki, we've been waiting for you!" said Old Man Saburo.

Actually, they had started drinking without him.

Iwao filled more glasses. Yoki set Granny Shige down on the tatami and lost no time joining in the fun.

"This is a Christmas party, isn't it?" Granny Shige said to Seiichi. "Thank you kindly for the invitation."

Meanwhile, Santa and I were going back and forth between the kitchen and the main room, helping to carry in platters of food till the big table was filled to overflowing. Their work finished, the women removed their aprons and sat down around the table.

"Nao phoned to say she has to stay and work late," Risa reported. Everyone agreed that schoolteachers had a hard job and marveled at Nao's devotion to her work.

"Well, let's get started without her," Seiichi said, and lightly raised his glass. "Thanks, everybody, for joining Santa and us for a Christmas celebration. Cheers!"

"Cheers!" Santa and I touched glasses. He was drinking orange juice, but everybody else, including Granny Shige, drank beer. Kamusari women can hold their liquor. Normally they don't drink much, but at festivals and banquets, "the sake barrel has no bottom," as the saying goes.

Risa was saying, "I made lots of ice," and Miho, arms folded, responded, "Let's have *shochu* next." They weren't holding back.

All the food was good, although without Nao's contribution, vegetables were in short supply. Santa blissfully munched on fried chicken.

"What did you ask Santa Claus for?" I asked him.

"The Vegetable Squadron's Miracle Galactica-form Vegetable Robot!"

"Wow. What's that?"

"The Wonderful Vegetable Machine that the five members of the Vegetable Squadron ride changes into a giant robot. It's the final transformation."

Vegetable? Like, cabbage and stuff? Was the Vegetable Squadron strong? I had no idea. "Sounds amazing."

"And guess what! After I wrote to Santa asking for the Miracle Galactica-form Vegetable Robot, he wrote back!"

"No. Really?"

"I'll go get the letter. Wait here."

Santa flew out of the room. His footsteps grew fainter down the corridor, then louder again, and then he was back beside me.

"Here." He held out a bright green envelope. On the front it said "TO SANTA" in big letters. The writing resembled Seiichi's, I thought, but on the back of the envelope, in smaller lettering, it said "From Santa."

"Go ahead and read it," Santa said.

I pulled out a sheet of stationery the same color as the envelope. On it was this message:

> Dear Santa,
> Thank you for your letter. I'm glad you are well. I see you and I have the same name.
> I understand your desire for the Miracle Galactica-form Vegetable Robot. However, I am sorry to say

Shion Miura

I cannot deliver any present to you. You live in the remotest district of Kamusari village. Even in my sleigh pulled by reindeer, it would take a very long time for me to get there. On December 24, I have to travel around the world delivering presents to children, some of whom have nothing to eat and nowhere to live. I want to make those children my priority. (A "priority" is what you put first.) Therefore, please accept a present from your father instead.

Wishing you happiness with all my heart,

Santa

"See? See? Isn't it great?"

"Um, yeah!" Caught up in his enthusiasm, I nodded as I handed the letter back to him. "So did your daddy give you the whatchamacallit robot?"

"Uh-uh." He shook his head. "Here's what he gave me, instead. *Ta-da!*" He pulled out from behind his back . . . a foot-tall robot carved from wood. "It's a Miracle Galactica-form Vegetable Robot that Daddy made himself!"

"That's original."

Santa, what a sweet kid you are! Looking at his excited face, I felt my eyes grow hot. *Your daddy tricked you, Santa.* The robot Seiichi came up with hadn't cost him anything. It was made of wood, not shiny metal, and here in Kamusari, you could find wood in your sleep.

Not that price was the issue. That I understood. The hand-carved robot was painted in vivid colors: red for the head, green for the torso, orange for the right arm, purple for the left arm, and brown for the legs. Santa informed me that this was a faithful representation of Vegetable Squadron colors. All the corners had been filed down, and they were smooth to the touch. Also, there were screws at the joints so they

160

actually moved. It was an extremely classy wooden toy. Seiichi must have spent hours making it for Santa with infinite care.

Even so . . . it screamed "fake." If I'd been Santa, and I got a wooden robot like this when I'd been hoping for a Chogokin toy made of die-cast metal, I'd have been gutted and thrown a tantrum.

Santa laid the robot carefully on his lap and started to eat some chirashizushi. What a good heart he has! Not because he's spent his whole life in the village. It's his own innate character, and Risa and Seiichi's parenting.

Yoki, who was now guzzling sake like water, spotted Santa's robot. "What's this? Looks like you've got something pretty nice there, Santa."

"Daddy made it for me."

"Hoo-ee! Your daddy's pretty clever. Look, the arms and legs all move around in a circle. Here's a punch!"

"Quit it, Yoki! Give it back!"

They started playing together with the robot. The toy's fakeness didn't bother Yoki a bit. He actually seemed jealous that Santa had one and he didn't.

Noko, down in the earthen entryway, put his front paws on the edge of the raised floor near us and sniffed. I went down and gave him the dog food Yoki had brought along. It couldn't be fun for Noko to watch us eat all that good food while he had nothing, after all.

Seiichi put some braised pork belly on Granny Shige's plate and broke it up for her with chopsticks. Risa and Miho were in stitches, laughing like a pair of junior-high-school girls. Old Man Saburo and Iwao were drinking shochu while talking about how tomatoes are good for lowering blood pressure.

Iwao's wife teased: "Dear, you never eat tomatoes and you know it!"

None of it was the least Christmassy, but everyone seemed to be having a good time. I looked at the old wall clock. It was after seven thirty.

"Nao's kinda late, isn't she?"

At first I thought I must have spoken aloud without realizing it. But no, the speaker was Iwao. He had brought up Nao to move on from tomatoes after his wife's gentle barb.

"Maybe there's too much snow on the road and she can't ride her motorcycle," said Old Man Saburo.

"Yuki, take my pickup," said Yoki. "Drive over and get her."

I was ready to leave pronto, but Seiichi stopped me. "You've been drinking, haven't you?"

Ah. So I had.

"Let's wait a little more," said Risa cheerfully. "I baked a cake, so have some, everybody."

She went into the kitchen and brought out a whole cake, lavishly topped with whipped cream and strawberries. If I was going to hand out the presents I'd brought, now was the time. I'd rather give Nao hers when we were alone, anyway.

"Ahem." I stood up. "I brought presents for Santa, Granny Shige, Yoki, and Miho. I'm sorry I don't have enough for everyone."

"That's okay, that's okay!" Old Man Saburo clapped his hands. "Yuki went to a lot of trouble picking these out in Nagoya, everybody."

"Let's see them," said Iwao encouragingly, so I passed the presents out.

Santa carefully opened his, and when he saw the gloves, he shouted out, "Wow, these are cool! They've got stars on them. Like yours, Granny Shige!"

"So they do," she said. "Oh, these are nice and warm." She put them on and held her hands up admiringly in front of her face.

"What a lovely color these rice bowls are!" Miho's eyes sparkled. "The one Yoki uses is chipped. Starting tomorrow, we'll use these."

"They're nice." Yoki nodded. "Look like they'll hold plenty of rice." His eye fell on the bag I had brought. "Hey, there's one more present in there. Whose could it be?"

You know perfectly well. Damn you, Yoki.

"Leave the poor boy alone," said Old Man Saburo, and Yoki chuckled.

Everyone thanked me for their presents, and I nodded in return. I was glad they were a hit.

The cake was now cut, and we each had a piece. It was super-good. Risa could have sold it in a bakery, I thought. The sponge cake was beautifully light, with whipped cream not just on top but between the layers, and packed with strawberries. Santa dove into his and ended up with whipped cream around his mouth, like a mustache and beard.

Yoki laughed. "Look! Santa is Santa!"

Everybody agreed the cake was delicious. "Cake like this is hard to come by in Kamusari," somebody said.

"How did you bake it?" asked Miho. "Using the oven feature of your microwave?"

"No," said Risa. "Our microwave is old, and the oven temperature control doesn't work, so I baked it in the old wood stove."

"Sounds like a challenge."

"I wasn't sure how to adjust the fire. I messed up the first time." She laughed with embarrassment. "The second time, Seiichi kept an eye on the fire for me, so it went well. Thanks, dear."

The perfect husband and father! Just as well Nao wasn't there to be reminded.

Santa finished his cake and, tummy full, began nodding off.

"I thought this might happen, so I had him take an early bath." Risa sighed. "Santa, time to brush your teeth and go to bed."

"I wanna stay up," he said, but he could hardly keep his eyes open.

The wall clock said it was just past eight o'clock. He still maintained his schedule of "early to bed, early to rise," I noted, impressed.

"I'll go with you, Santa," I said, and he nodded. He told everyone good night and went off down the corridor, wearing his gloves and clutching his robot and the letter from Santa Claus. I followed behind.

Seiichi's house is very old and big. The corridor was dim and chilly, and it went on and on, twisting and turning. I found it a bit unnerving, to tell the truth. Santa, who was used to it, walked along without fear, even half asleep.

The sink where he brushed his teeth was in the deep recesses of the house. It occurred to me that if we got separated, I might not be able to find my way back, but fortunately Santa's bedroom was fairly close to the main room.

He went into the bedroom, turned on the light, and changed into his pajamas. He still had the gloves on, so this took a little time. His futon was already laid out.

"You always sleep alone?"

"Yeah, ever since I started school."

"Good for you. You don't get lonesome, all by yourself?"

"Nope. But sometimes I do go get into my parents' futon," he added shyly.

"You gonna sleep with those gloves on?"

"Yeah."

"Your hands might get too hot."

"I don't care. I really like them. Thanks, Yu-chan."

"You're welcome. Okay, lights out."

"Leave the night-light on."

"Got it. Like this? Good night."

"G'night."

He snuggled into bed under the pale orange night-light. I left his room and gently closed the door.

Through a corridor window I saw snow falling on the yard. And then, slicing through the darkness, the headlights of an approaching car. At first I thought it must be her motorcycle, but no. It was a white sedan. She got out of the passenger seat, smiling; said something to the driver; then walked across the snow toward Seiichi's front door. The car backed up, turned around, and went out into the road.

164

I automatically took a step forward—and smacked my forehead on the windowpane. It hurt, but something else bothered me more.

I ran down the corridor, through the main room where the party was still going on, and down into the entryway. I stuck my feet in a pair of sandals while Yoki and the rest, including Noko, looked at me, puzzled. Paying them no mind, I threw open the front door and bumped into Nao, who'd been trying to open it from the other side.

"Oh, Yuki! You surprised me!" She smiled at me as she stepped inside. "Sorry I'm late. I brought salad, but maybe everybody's done eating?"

"Nao," I said, "was that Okuda in the car just now? You should have invited him in."

Her expression stiffened. "How do you know his name? Did I ever introduce you?"

"No, but it was easy to find out."

"Was it now." She said this in a voice as cold as that of *yuki-onna*, the snow woman of folklore. Behind her, a gust of wind blew snow through the open door. "That wasn't Mr. Okuda's car. Just as I was getting my bike out, Mrs. Yamane from next door came by on her way home from work. She gave me a ride because it was on her way and she didn't think I'd be safe on a motorcycle in this snow."

Shit. I could feel the blood drain from my face. Nao was quietly furious. Her icy gaze went straight through me with the power of a hundred yuki-onna.

"So that's what you think of me? That I'm just a flirt? That on Christmas Eve, knowing how you feel about me, I would get a male colleague to drive me here and rub it in your face?"

"I didn't mean that." But her accusation was spot-on. That was exactly what I'd thought. I'd been blindly jealous. "I-I'm sorry."

Nao scoffed (her scoffing dripped icicles), slipped past me, and joined the others.

The room was silent. Yoki had been listening so intently, he'd lost his balance. He was lying on the floor.

"Sorry I'm late," she said, smiling. "Risa, here's the salad. Save it and have it tomorrow." She took out three Tupperware containers from her backpack and handed them to Risa. One was potato salad, I saw, one was lettuce and cucumber, and one was fruit salad.

I slunk into a corner and sat with my head down.

"Thanks," said Risa. With a worried glance at me, she took the containers. "You haven't eaten, have you, Nao? There's cake, too, you know."

"No, thanks. I'll pass. I'm tired, so I think I'll just turn in. Seiichi, I'll borrow the usual room, if that's okay."

"Absolutely."

Nao turned to everyone. "Good night, all." She studiously avoided my eyes. Then she left.

The moment her footsteps reached the top of the stairs, the room broke into a hubbub.

"Now that was Yuki's fault," said Granny Shige.

Miho was indignant. "Why didn't he apologize more? He doesn't understand a woman's heart."

"I've been so busy teaching him about forestry," said Yoki, "I never taught him how to get along with the ladies." He was now sitting up again. He folded his arms with an air of importance.

Hah. Yoki always says, "Learn by doing," and never teaches me anything properly.

Iwao turned to his wife. "So Yuki's still going for Nao? He hasn't given up?"

She said, "If he did, there wouldn't be anyone his age in the village for him to make a match with."

That wasn't why I'd fallen for Nao.

Seiichi and Risa, as relatives of one of the parties involved, looked concerned but said nothing.

Old Man Saburo set his glass on the table with a clatter. "Yuki. What do you think love is?"

"Huh?" Was I supposed to make some sort of declaration here? As I shrank back, Old Man Saburo shook his head as if to say, *Honestly, young folks nowadays.*

He began talking in a quiet voice. All eyes were on him, mine, too. "My father was a shameless womanizer."

"That he was," Granny Shige agreed. "That man didn't have to say a word. Women swarmed around him. Why, next to him, Yoki'd have to run away barefoot and hide his face. That's how much of a playboy the man was."

"Anybody who's got me beat must be a regular demon," said Yoki, clearly impressed.

What a thing to boast about!

"After the war," said Old Man Saburo, "he'd go into town and chase after women. Me and my little brother were kids, but we'd see our mother crying, and we felt bad for her."

Iwao said, "I always knew you never cheated on your wife. Must be because your father set you an example of what not to do."

Iwao's wife turned to him. "Well, now. Judging from the way you said that, I take it you've cheated on *your* wife a time or two."

"No, no!" he protested. "Never!"

Ignoring this interruption, Old Man Saburo went on. "But one day, he gave up chasing women. Instead, he began furiously chopping wood."

Chopping wood? Whatever for? Puzzled, I cocked my head.

"In those days, we still used a wood-burning stove. We needed firewood to cook food and heat the bath. He piled up a huge amount of firewood all around the house and filled the storehouse to bursting, too. He even repaired the outhouse floor while he was at it. My mother thought it was strange, but she was happy about the change. Chopping wood and piling it up is hard work for a woman."

"Your pa was a touch different from others," murmured Granny Shige. "He had what you might call a strong intuition."

"That's so." Old Man Saburo lowered his voice. "He'd tell Mother, 'Get out my black mourning clothes, and don't let on to anyone.' Within three days there'd be a death in the village, sure as I'm sitting here."

He was psychic? Isn't that a bit creepy? That's what I thought, but everybody else was nodding, like *Yeah, that could happen.* Kamusari is full of surprises. I decided not to probe into it.

"After he'd chopped so much firewood there was no more place to put it, one day he died in the mountains. He'd been fine the day before, but his heart gave out." Old Man Saburo's voice took on a somber tone. "He knew his time was near. That's why he chopped so much firewood, so Mother would be able to cook and heat water long after he was gone. I looked at those mountains of firewood, and I said to myself, *This is what real love looks like.*"

I wasn't so sure. After chasing women all he likes, one day he keels over. Just because he'd chopped a lot of firewood ahead of time, would that incline his wife to forgive him? I didn't think so.

Yoki expressed his own doubt. "The firewood would shrink day by day, though, right? I don't know about a form of love that slowly vanishes."

"Naa-naa," said Old Man Saburo.

The essential part of his story he summed up with the village watchword, meaning, in this case, "Don't worry about it. Never mind the details."

"Mother complained, too," he said. "I remember she said, *I was just thinking I'd switch to propane and buy an electric stove. Now I'll have to use up all this firewood first.*"

And so it was a long time before Old Man Saburo's family had switched to gas heating and an electric stove. Love can really be inconvenient.

Miho had been listening silently. Now she issued this conclusion: "Anyway, Yuki needs to apologize to Nao tomorrow. Don't tiptoe around it. There comes a time, for men and women both, when you have to lay it on the line."

"I'll lend you my pickup," said Yoki. "First thing in the morning, give Nao a ride home. I'll hitch a ride to work with Seiichi. Yuki'll join us a little late, but that's all right, isn't it, Seiichi?"

"That's fine." Seiichi then announced that the party was over. "It looks like tomorrow will be a day of decision for Yuki. Let's not drink too much, and call it a night."

Okay, but the floor was already littered with big, empty bottles of sake.

Noko, lying with his face buried in his front paws, wagged his tail at Seiichi's announcement.

The next morning, I got in Yoki's pickup and drove over to pick Nao up. Just in case, I took along the present I had failed to give her the night before.

When I left the house, Miho handed me my lunch (Yoki, by the way, was still asleep). "Today's onigiri is stuffed with pork cutlet," she said. "I got up early and made it for you, so do your best and win the day."

She meant well, but her words increased the pressure.

Before school, Nao needed to stop off at her house to get ready. It was six o'clock, too early for the team's morning meeting. Only the red pine, wearing a cotton hat, served as a reminder of the party.

When Nao came to the door, she seemed cross—no surprise there.

"Good morning," I said.

"Morning."

"I'm really sorry I jumped to the wrong conclusion yesterday."

"Never mind."

What should I do? She was hardly talking to me. After getting in the passenger seat, she stared silently and balefully ahead.

It had stopped snowing during the night, and asphalt showed through the tire tracks in the road. But melting snow is slippery. I held the steering wheel with care and drove slowly—partly because I wanted as much time as possible to set things straight.

Kamusari is deep in the mountains, and dawn was a long way off. Lit up by the headlights, the surface of the snow twinkled like stars. The pickup proceeded down the narrow, cedar-lined road. Time to live up to my name. *Come on!* I urged myself. *Work up your courage and tell her!*

"I've been jealous of your coworker Okuda for a long time. I saw you in his car that time, and I knew you were together at work, and I'm younger than you are."

The minute I said all this, I knew how pitiful it sounded. *Come on! Don't just gripe at her!*

"I already knew you were small and jealous."

It was true, but did she have to say it so matter-of-factly? Ouch.

"I won't get jealous from now on. I'll be careful."

A big clump of snow slid off cedar branches overhead and landed *kerplop* on the windshield. We both jumped, and I turned on the windshield wipers. Nao said something, but the wipers made so much noise, I missed it. *Yoki, change the rubber on your windshield wipers already!*

I turned the wipers off. "What did you say?"

"I said you're a coward. You avoided having a Christmas for just the two of us, so now why all this fuss?"

Whaat! Was *that* what bothered her? When I called to invite her to the party, she'd sounded kind of evasive. Was it because she felt let down that I hadn't asked her on a Christmas date? No, impossible. I was making too much out of this, indulging in wishful thinking. My heart pounded.

"You know what really gets to me?" She folded her arms.

Uh-oh. Before she'd said, "Never mind," but she was still mad, after all. When a woman says, "Never mind," you can't take it literally; I knew that much. To show her I was listening, I slowed down even more.

"It's not that you were jealous. It's that even though you like me enough to *be* jealous, you don't trust me the least little bit."

"Yeah, but that's . . ."

"What?"

"I *want* to trust you, but I worry."

"Why?"

"Because I've told you over and over how I feel about you, but you've never said how you feel about me. I can't help going around in circles in my mind."

"Then if I said I liked you, you'd stop going around in circles?"

"You like me!"

"I said *if* I liked you."

There you go again. I had turned to look at her, but now, disappointed, I looked straight ahead again. "I know the answer," I said. "Say you'll be my girlfriend."

"Why is that the answer?"

"Even if you say you like me and even if you agree to be my girlfriend, I'm pretty sure I'll still go around in circles and I'll still get jealous. I'm crazy about you. I can't help it. But it would set my mind at ease, give me confidence, to know you were my girlfriend. Getting jealous even though you're not, even though I have no claim on you at all, really does make me feel small and . . . what's the word? Pitiful."

"I know that feeling." Nao had the experience of being jealous of her sister. She nodded soberly.

"Right? So if you like me even a little, go ahead and say you'll be my girlfriend. Set my mind at ease. Then if it turns out you can't stand me and I give you the willies, we can always break up."

"I can't decide if you're pushy or groveling."

I glanced over. She was laughing. She was adorable. Truly.

Then it came to me: if I knew I was going to die, I'd be like Old Man Saburo's father and do everything in my power for Nao, try to make her happy.

Wanting someone to be happy after you die. Wanting to spend the time until you die with them: eating supper and heating the bath and quarreling like always. Just as Old Man Saburo said, that is surely what love is. It makes me a little shy to write it.

Coming to Kamusari and getting to know the people here, living with them and working alongside them, has taught me about life and love. The villagers plant trees that will be harvested a hundred years in the future; they cut down trees their ancestors planted long ago. They know that just as they spend their days laughing and getting angry, so did people a hundred years ago, and so will people a hundred years on. They go on tending the forests on the mountains around Kamusari, praying for the happiness of those who will survive them and those who are yet to be born. That, I think, is real faith and real love.

Of course, there was faith and love in Yokohama, too. I was just too young to see it. My father going to work every day, earning money to support the family. My mother, scolding us and pulling some pretty crazy stunts, but always caring about my brother and me. My brother, falling in love and getting married and becoming a father, and all the relatives who dote on his kid. Things like that happen all around, all over the place.

Even if the world were ending tomorrow, you couldn't suddenly beat up on people close to you. Faith and love are in our DNA. We're programmed to feel optimism and hope that tomorrow, and the day after, and a hundred years from now, people will still live happily. We have the strength to live with that future happiness in mind, headed in that direction. That's why it's so painful to come across someone who, for whatever reason, has lost sight of faith and love, given in to despair.

Of course, when you really think about it, there's no guarantee whatsoever that the future a hundred years from now will arrive without a hitch. Hoping it will is actually nuts, in a way.

What am I talking about? I'm not used to thinking about things on so grand a scale. I've kind of lost the thread.

Anyway, I want Nao to be happy. Even if we break up, or I die, or we never see each other again, I want her to be happy with all my heart. I didn't know I was capable of feeling this way. She and Kamusari made me realize it. They taught me that faith and love do exist in the world, and inside me.

When I pulled up in front of Nao's house, she still hadn't answered my question.

"Thanks for the ride," she said and went in the house. I sat and watched her go. At least I had conveyed my feelings (though yet again without getting a commitment from her), so I decided to be happy with that. Then I remembered her present, still there beside me.

I turned off the engine and sat there waiting for her to emerge. The cold seeped in through the steel body of the truck, but it didn't really bother me.

After about twenty minutes, she appeared on the front doorstep. Today was the closing ceremony, so she was wearing a black suit with a knee-length skirt that showed off her slender, lithe legs. She had a heavy-looking bag slung over her shoulder, and she was wearing a black jacket, not a coat. Just what I would have expected.

Seeing me still parked there, she came over, looking dubious. I got out of the truck with the present in my hand.

"What's up?"

"I forgot to give you your Christmas present."

She took the package I held out. "May I open it?"

"By all means."

She unwrapped the package and softly stroked the red scarf. "What a pretty color!"

She looked up at me. Somehow, I don't know how, I knew what she wanted me to do. I took the scarf from her and wrapped it around her neck. And then I k-k-k-k-kissed her. Just lightly. It was morning, and there was no telling who might be watching.

"I don't want to make you worry," she whispered.

"Then be my girlfriend, starting today?"

"Do we *have* to put it into words that way, like a contract? It's not romantic." She laughed. Her cheeks were a little red. She was adorable.

I didn't know what else to do except ask her outright. Did she want our relationship to change little by little, instead of all at once? I was baffled—but judging from the expression on her face, she became my girlfriend in that moment, for real. I thanked the gods of Kamusari.

"Oh, no, I'll be late!" She got on her Kawasaki. Pretty bold, considering she was wearing a skirt, I thought, but then I saw she had on knee supporters. *Sorry for looking. My eyes traveled there of their own accord.*

As she started her engine, I said, "The tag's still on your scarf!"

"I'll take it off when I get there. It's all right."

I took advantage of the confusion of the moment to ask the next question: "Can I claim the right of *medo*?"

Nao was just putting on her helmet. She froze.

The right of medo is given to the man who plays a leading role in the grand festival of Oyamazumi-san, the god of Kamusari. The grand festival takes place just once every forty-eight years, most recently last year. (This year's festival, where they felled the chestnut tree and transported it out by helicopter, wasn't the grand festival, but the regular Oyamazumi festival.)

And as for what sort of right it is . . . it's the right to ask a woman you like to sleep with you. In other words, I'd come out and told Nao, "I love you, so I want us to be really, *really* intimate." Yikes.

Shyness, hope, and nervousness turned me into an ice statue as I waited for her to answer. After an eternity, she said, "Don't be an idiot.

After work, call me." She put on her helmet, smiled at me with her eyes, and took off, cutting a dashing figure.

As if the ice encasing me were melting away, sweat started pouring from every pore in my body. My ears hadn't played tricks on me, had they? *Call me call me call me* . . . the words reverberated endlessly in my mind.

Oh, man! I wanted to shout out for joy and jump up and down, but my excitement and happiness were so intense I couldn't move. I stood there like a statue.

I think I got pretty sunburned.

What happened after that, you ask? I'll leave it to your imagination.

I went home to Yokohama for New Year's, and Nao stayed with her folks in Tokyo from January 3 until the day before the start of the new term, so even though we just started going together, we've hardly seen each other.

Ever since my return from Yokohama, I've been writing this account, picking times when Granny Shige's not watching to tell about the Christmas party and how it turned out. Tomorrow night, Nao's coming back. Can't wait. She called not long ago, and we arranged for me to meet her at the station. Naturally, after I take her home, I have every intention of going on inside. Mwa-ha-ha.

When she called, Yoki answered the phone, so the news spread instantly through the house.

Granny Shige grinned and said, "A sleepover?"

Miho told me in no uncertain terms, "She's an unmarried woman, so see that you don't do anything to get people talking about her."

Yoki silently slipped a pack of condoms into my hand. *I have my own, thanks!*

"You and Nao, going together? Shows you've got guts." Yoki shook his head in apparent disbelief as we sat around the kotatsu at suppertime. "You'll be under her thumb."

I didn't need to hear that from him, of all people. Miho has him squarely under her thumb and he knows it.

I've been writing this after everybody went to bed, but just now Yoki slid open the door and came in. I quickly switched the computer to sleep mode.

"What's up?"

He sat down by me, looking serious for a change. "Yuki, what are your plans after this?"

"Plans?"

"Are you going to move into Nao's place and live with her?"

This took me by surprise. "No, no. It's way too soon for anything like that. I still have so much to learn about forestry. I'd like to stay on here a little longer and keep on learning from you."

"Oh, okay." His face relaxed into a smile. He must have been worried that I was getting ready to move out. "Good. You're still a beginner, after all, nowhere near a master of forestry. Watch me and tremble."

Why does he always have to lord it over me?

Yoki clapped a hand on my shoulder and then stood up. "You know," he said, "it's time you bought a pickup of your own. There's still a parking place available by the assembly hall. It's awfully inconvenient to be seeing a woman without your own set of wheels."

The voice of experience.

"I haven't saved up enough yet."

"Take out a loan from the Bank of Yoki."

"I bet the interest is high."

"Bah. Financing is flexible. Count on it." Yoki yawned and headed back into his bedroom. "We've got work tomorrow. Get some sleep."

He's right. I'll wrap up this account and go to bed.

What will happen tomorrow in the village and on the mountains? What shall I talk about with Nao when I see her? My brother's kid got really big; he understands what you say to him now. When I left Yokohama the first time, he was still crawling on all fours.

Nighttime in Kamusari is so quiet. All I can hear is Granny Shige's snoring next door. She's sore because I changed the password, so she can't sneak in and read this. She knows I use the name of someone important to me as the password, so you'd think she could guess I chose SHIGE.

Well, everybody, I think you must know this by now, but let me just say, I really love Kamusari. More than I ever thought I would. I've written down all I know about the place, its legends, and all the things that have happened here. I hope you all love Kamusari a little, too. That would make me glad.

Noko just sneezed outside. It's started snowing again. I hope it doesn't pile up too much. But Kamusari in the snow is beautiful, especially at night. The mountains and the bridge and the houses are all covered in white, with a pale glow. Only the Kamusari River is black, its surface reflecting myriad stars that twinkle like fragments of ice or lights in windows, each with its own rhythm.

Tomorrow I'll go up the mountain and tend the trees there. Before long, wood from Kamusari trees may end up where you are, as the pillars in your house, the furniture and chopsticks you use, or any of a hundred other things. When it does, think of Kamusari, and of us.

And someday, I'd love it if you came to visit. I'll be waiting!

And so, good night. Thanks for reading this!

ABOUT THE AUTHOR

Photo © Hiroyuki Matsukage

Shion Miura made her fiction debut in 2000 with *Kakuto suru mono ni maru* (*A Passing Grade for Those Who Fight*). In 2006, she won the Naoki Prize for her story collection *Mahoro ekimae Tada Benriken* (*The Handymen in Mahoro Town*). Her other novels include *Kaze ga tsuyoku fuiteiru* (*The Wind Blows Hard*), *Kogure-so monogatari* (*The Kogure Apartments*), and *Ano ie ni kurasu yonin no onna* (*The Four Women Living in That House*). Her other works in English, all translated by Juliet Winters Carpenter, include *The Easy Life in Kamusari* (*Kamusari naanaa nichijo*), volume one in her Forest series, and *The Great Passage* (*Fune o amu*), which was made into an award-winning motion picture and received both the Booksellers' Award in Japan in 2012 and an Earphones Award. Miura has also published more than fifteen collections of essays and is a manga aficionado.

ABOUT THE TRANSLATOR

Photo © 2014 Toyota Horiguchi

Juliet Winters Carpenter is a professor emerita of Doshisha Women's College of Liberal Arts. Her first translated novel, *Secret Rendezvous* by Kobo Abe, received the 1980 Japan-U.S. Friendship Commission Prize for the Translation of Japanese Literature. In 2014, her translation of *A True Novel* by Minae Mizumura received the same award. Besides Shion Miura's *The Great Passage* and two-volume Forest series, Carpenter's recent translations include Mizumura's *An I-Novel,* Keiichiro Hirano's *At the End of the Matinee,* and Tōru Haga's *Pax Tokugawana: The Cultural Flowering of Japan, 1603–1853.* Her forthcoming translations include Masatsugu Ono's *At the Edge of the Wood* and Kiyoko Murata's *A Woman of Pleasure.* Carpenter lives on Whidbey Island in Washington State.